Nee

NEEDING GHOSTS

Ramsey Campbell

Illustrated by Jamel Akib

CENTURY

A LEGEND NOVELLA

LONDON SYDNEY AUCKLAND JOHANNESBURG

Copyright © 1990 by Ramsey Campbell

Illustrations © 1990 by Jamel Akib
Legend Novellas: all cover design by Steve Ridgeway, Splash Studio

A Legend novella published by Century

First published in Great Britain by Random Century Group
20 Vauxhall Bridge Road, London SW1V 2SA

Century Hutchinson South Africa (Pty) Ltd
PO Box 337, Bergvlei 2012, South Africa

Random Century Australia Pty Ltd
20 Alfred Street, Milsons Point, Sydney, NSW 2061
Australia

Random Century New Zealand Ltd
PO Box 40–086, Glenfield, Auckland 10
New Zealand

A CIP Catalogue Record for this book is available from the
British Library

ISBN 0 7126 3691 9 (hardcover) 0 7126 2159 8 (paperback)

Typeset by Selectmove Ltd, London
Printed and bound in Great Britain by
Mackays of Chatham PLC, Chatham, Kent

My wife Jenny was invaluable as always, though she didn't think this book as comic as I did. I'm grateful to John Mottershead of the Chapter One bookshop in Liverpool for the loan of his surname, and I've a special thank-you for Deborah Beale, my editor at Legend, without whose encouragement *Needing Ghosts* would never have been written.

For Penny and Alan
and Timmy and Robin
— some of my dark to find your ways through

He knows this dark. Though it feels piled against his eyes, it doesn't mean he's blind. He only has to lie there until he can tell where he is. As soon as his sense of his body returns he'll know which way he's lying.

He feels as though he has forgotten how to close his eyes and how to breathe. Perhaps he could shout and gain some idea of the extent of his surroundings from whatever happens to his voice, but he can't think of anything to say. The notion of shouting without words dismays him, and so does the possibility that he mightn't know what he means to shout until he hears himself.

In any case, his sense of himself is beginning to gather. His arms are stretched out parallel to his body, his hands lie palms downwards by his sides. How thin they are! He's disinclined to raise them to his eyes in case he's unable to see them. The darkness must relent eventually, and meanwhile there's no call for him to move; didn't he take some trouble to achieve this peace? Now that he's aware of the remainder of his body – the outstretched legs, the upturned toes, the tight skin over the ribs – he ought to be able to enjoy lying still.

But the darkness is no longer absolute. It has begun to betray hints of shapes standing tall and immobile as if they're waiting to be seen. Those directly ahead of him appear to be draped in robes, and can't he hear voices whispering? He thinks of judges watching him with eyes that pierce the blackness, judges waiting for the dawn to reveal them and himself.

To his right he can just distinguish the profile of an open box at least as tall as himself. Hovering within it is an object which looks too oddly proportioned to be complete. To his left is an open horizontal box, from which shapes dangle as though exhausted by their struggle to emerge. He very much hopes that the whispers aren't coming from either box.

His clenched fists spread their fingers and reach out shakily on either side of him. By stretching his arms to their limit he can grasp the edges of the lumpy creaking mattress, and the action gives him some awareness of the room. Those aren't robed figures ahead of him, they're heavy curtains, and he's almost sure that if he parts them to admit more light he'll see that the figure hovering in the wardrobe, the stumps of its legs drawn up towards its handless monkey arms, is nothing of the kind.

He drags his hands over the mattress, the twang and contour and inclination of each buried spring reviving that much of his memory. He digs his knuckles into the frayed canvas and lifts himself into a sitting position, then he swings his legs into the dark and inches them downwards until his feet touch the floor. The carpet is so worn he can distinguish the outlines of the floorboards. Pushing himself away from the bed, he pads to the curtains, beyond which he can hear the whispering. He pokes his fingers through the gap in the musty velvet and heaves the curtains back.

The night is dancing just beyond the grimy window. Poplars whose foliage the dark has transmuted into coal toss their long heads in the wind. Several yards below him, wind ploughs through the grass of an unkempt garden hemmed in by trees. Inside the window, at the bottom left-hand corner of the lower sash, a draught plucks at a stray leaf caught in a spider's glimmering web.

So much for the whispering, however nearly articulate it sounds. He turns to the room. His suit is on a single hanger in the wardrobe, other clothes of his spill out of the chest of drawers. He isn't used to waking by himself in the dark, that's all. Now that he has risen he'll stay up and be on his way by dawn.

He trots out of the room and along the threadbare corridor without switching on the light above the stairs. When he tugs the cord in the bathroom, the light-bulb greets its own reflection in the mirror full of white tiles, and something disappears into the plughole of the bruised bath. It must be a drip from the taps whose marble eyeballs bulge above their brass snout; he sees the movement glisten as it vanishes. He crosses the knotted floor and confronts himself in the mirror.

'There you are, old thinface. Nothing wrong with you that a blade can't put right.' He's being deliberately cheerful, because he has never cared for the way electric light looks at this hour – too bright, as if its glare is straining to fend off the dark, and yet too feeble. His face resembles a paper mask, the skin almost smooth except for furrows underlining the sparse shock of grey hair, and almost white save for touches of pink in the twin hollows of the pinched cheeks, in the large nostrils of the long nose, on the pursed lips. The stubble on the pointed chin makes him feel grimy, and he ransacks the clutter by the sink for a razor.

Most of the stuff there seems to have nothing to do with him. At last he finds a razor folded into its handle among the sticky jars. He digs his thumbnail into the crescent-shaped nick in the blade, which springs out so readily that he can't help flinching. What's become of his electric razor? It's posing as another jar, its heads clogged by talcum powder. On second thoughts, his chin can stay as it is. He stoops to the sink and wets his face with water from the right-hand tap, which grumbles like a sleeping animal, then he dries himself on a towel with a hole in it the size of his face. He lets down the dark with the cord and hurries to his room.

This time he switches on the light above the bed. The walls absorb much of the glow of the dim unshaded bulb, as their blurred surface seems already to have assimilated the pattern and the colours of the paper. Though the room is spacious, it contains little furniture: the open wardrobe, the overflowing chest of drawers, the double bed with the bare mattress whose stripes trace the unevenness of the springs – just enough, he thinks, to show that it's a bedroom. He lifts his suit from the hanger and picks up the shoes which stand beneath it as though they've fallen from the legs. Once he is dressed he tours the house.

He shuts the lid of the massive toilet and rubs his hands with the ragged towel, and slams the bathroom door. Between it and his room are two bedrooms, an unmade single bed in each. Light through the lampshades steeps his hands in red as he fingers the wall-sockets to reassure himself that they're switched off. As he backs out of each room he turns the light off and shuts the door, holding onto the doorknob until he feels the lock click.

The clatter of his shoes on the uncarpeted staircase tells him how empty the large house is, and reminds him that he doesn't mean it to be empty for much longer. When he has opened the bookshop and customers are selling books to him as well as buying them, he'll store part of his stock in the disused bedrooms. He strides along the L-shaped hall to the kitchen, where fluorescent light smoulders in its tube while he screws the gas taps tight and grovels on the flagstones to examine the electric sockets on the perspiring brownish walls. He needn't check the room next to the kitchen, since it's locked. He looks into the rooms which, once their shared wall is removed, will house the shop. Chairs lean against a dining-table beneath the one live bulb of a chandelier, a lounge suite squats in front of a television tethered to a video recorder. He shuts the doors and lifts his rucksack from the post at the foot of the stairs. Hitching the rucksack over his shoulders, he lets himself out of the house.

The wind has dropped. The poplars are embedded in the tarry sky. Before he reaches the end of his overgrown path and steps into the avenue, his greenish shoes are black with dew. The road leads downhill between buildings which gleam white beyond the trees. Glancing back to reassure himself that he hasn't left a light on by mistake, he sees that all his windows are dark, all the curtains are open except those of the locked room.

He isn't surprised to find himself alone on the road; presumably nobody else rises at this hour. He can't recall ever having met his neighbours, but if they want to avoid him, that suits him. 'He's out again,' he announces at the top of his voice. 'Lock your doors, hide behind the furniture, pull the blankets over your heads or he'll know you're there.'

The only response, if it is a response, is the flight of a bird which starts up from among the trees and passes overhead, invisibly black, with a sound like the sweeps of a scythe. When it has gone and he falls silent, he thinks he can hear dew dripping in the trees beside the road. Spider threads caress his face, and he imagines the night as a web in the process of being assembled. He halts on the crown of the tarmac, wondering whether, if he's still enough, he may hear the whisper of the threads. Disturbed by the idea – not so much by the possibility of hearing as by his compulsion to try – he hurries down the avenue, wishing his tread were louder. He's glad when the landing-stage becomes visible at the end of the road.

Perhaps he's too early. Though a ferry is moored there, it's unlit. As he continues downhill, the lights across the bay appear to sink into the black water. Just as he emerges between the last of the poplars, the lights vanish, and he feels as if everything – sky, trees, land, sea – has merged into a single lightless medium. The anchorage creaks as he picks his way to the gangplank and steps onto the deck.

All the stairways to the upper deck are roped off, and the doors of the saloons are locked. He's heading along the narrow strip of deck beside the front saloon when the gangplank is raised with a rattle of chains and the ferry gives a honk which vibrates through the boards underfoot. At once, as if the sound has started the waves up, water slops against the hull as the vessel swings out from the stage.

If it weren't for the occasional creak which reminds him of the sounds a house emits at night, he would hardly know he was on a boat. By the time the engine begins to thump, the ferry is well out from the shore. From the upper deck he would presumably be able to see the lights of his destination. He grips the sides of the prow and thrusts himself forwards like a figurehead, but can't determine whether the unsteady glow which appears to divide the blackness ahead is real or if it's only the flickering which often manifests itself within his eyelids when he can't sleep. He wedges his thighs in the V of the prow and watches the forest swallowing the buildings on the avenue. He finds the sight oddly satisfying, and so he doesn't face forwards again until the ferry has almost gained the opposite side of the bay. When the steersman, a bust illuminated like a waxwork by the instruments in the wheelhouse, closes down the engine, he slips out of his niche in the prow and turns to look.

The landing-stage is wider than the one below the poplars. Several figures are rising from benches in a shed at the back of the stage. Floodlights bleach the planks and show him the

faces of those waiting – flesh white as candles, eyes like glass –
as they crowd to meet him at the gangplank. He sidles past the
crewman who has let the gangplank down, a burly man whose
black beard so resembles the fabric of his Balaclava that his
eyes and nose look false, and hurries across the shed to the
exit ramp.

Only one of the several pay booths at the top of the tunnel is
occupied. The woman inside it is poring over an obese dog-
eared paperback, its cover hanging open to display a resale
stamp. She waits until he pushes a pound coin under the glass
of the booth before she raises her flat sleepy face, and he
thinks of slot machines in the seaside arcades of his child-
hood, glass booths containing puppets which tottered alive if
one fed them a coin. He's heading for the exit when she swivels on her stool and raps on the glass with the largest wedding
ring he has ever seen. 'Hey!'

If the fare has gone up, the least she can do is tell him by
how much. But she only stares at him and thrusts her hand
under the glass, and he thinks she's pointing at him until he
notices the coin beneath her fingers. 'Too rich to need
your change?' she says.

'You've only taken for me.'

'That's right, unless you're hiding someone in your bag.'

'There's the bicycle.'

She stares as if she's refusing to acknowledge a joke,
though she can see perfectly well what he means. He gestures
at the barrier where he leaned the machine when she called
him back, and then he realizes with a shock that he has left
the bicycle at home. When he apologizes and reaches for
the coin, her fingers recoil like caterpillars, and she bends
the paperback open so fiercely that the bunch of pages she
has read loses its grip on the spine and falls inside the booth.
He knees the barrier aside and marches out of the tunnel,
wondering what else he may have forgotten, feeling as though
his very substance has been undermined.

On the far side of a broad deserted road, concrete office
buildings catch fragments of the white glare of streetlamps
in their multitude of windows. The interiors of the double-
decker buses parked in a layby opposite the ferry terminal look
moonlit. All six bus-stops have someone waiting at them.

As he crosses the whitened tarmac, the six men watch him silently. All of them are wearing dark suits – black, unless the light is altering the colour of their clothes as much as it's discolouring their faces. They don't respond when he nods to them, and so he does his best to ignore them while he looks for information. The timetables have been wrenched off the bus-stops; even the numbers on the metal flags have been rendered unidentifiable by graffiti which turns sevens into nines, nines into eights, whole numbers into mixed. Computer displays on the fronts of the vehicles announce destinations, but they bewilder him. Are the computers malfunctioning? Flicky Doaky, Eyes End, Cranium, Roly Polytechnic, View Hallow, Pearly Swine – he doesn't believe there are any such places; perhaps the names are jokes the drivers crack after the buses stop running. The men by the bus-stops seem to be waiting for him to react, and he can't help suspecting that they're drivers. He leans against a building to wait for someone to board a bus.

The men turn away from him and exchange glances, and begin to call out to one another. 'I'll be gone as soon as I get my head down.'

'I'll have mine under the covers before the sun's up.'

'Nothing like sleeping when the world's abroad.'

'Nothing worse than not being able to switch yourself off.'

'You mean the poor bat who couldn't even when he was supposed to have retired.'

'And wouldn't let anyone else.'

It sounds like a prepared routine, passing systematically along the line from right to left, and he feels as if they're talking at him. He's beginning to experience a rage so black it suffocates his words when another man emerges from a crevice beside him, an alley between the buildings. This one must be a driver, though he is almost a dwarf; he's wearing the uniform. He toddles to the second bus from the left and turns a knob which folds the door open, and it seems clear that he's the person to ask. 'Excuse me . . .'

The driver pokes a finger under the brim of his cap. Thick spectacles make his eyes appear to occupy the top half of his wizened face. 'Not open yet. You don't see anyone else moving.'

True enough, all the dark-suited figures have turned

towards the conversation and are frozen in attitudes of listening; some have lifted their hands to their ears. 'I only wanted to ask which bus goes to—'

He can't remember. With the loss of the word, his mind seems to shrink and darken. The driver is waiting as though only the word will release him, raising his eyebrows until his eyes fill the lenses of his spectacles. At last a name rises out of the dark. 'To Mottershead. Which bus goes to Mottershead?'

'Never heard of it,' the driver says triumphantly, and hops onto the bus. 'Nothing called that round here.'

'Of course there is.'

The door flattens into its frame, and he's about to thump on the fingermarked glass when he realizes that Mottershead isn't the name of a place: it's his own name. He retreats and presses his spine against the facade of an office in which typewriters are hooded like ranks of cowled heads. He's restraining himself from turning his face to the concrete when the driver, having hoisted himself into the seat behind the wheel, reopens the doors and inclines his torso towards him. 'Got another name for me?'

Mottershead thinks he sees a way out of the trap. 'Where do you go?'

'Where it says.'

Perhaps there really is a district called Eyes End. If Mottershead doesn't board the vehicle he'll be alone with five of the six men who witnessed his discomfiture, the sixth having flashed a rectangle of plastic at the driver and sat in the front downstairs seat. He watches Mottershead with interest and twirls a slow finger in one nostril. 'That'll do me,' Mottershead tells the driver, and steps onto the platform.

In his pocket is only a twenty-pound note and the change from the ferry. The driver reaches a long arm out of his metal enclosure and plucks the coin from Mottershead's hand. 'You'll hear me call when you've run out,' he warns, and starts the bus.

Mottershead is on the stairs when the vehicle backs at speed into the road and immediately lurches forward. He grabs the tubular banister and hauls himself to the top deck, where he lunges at the left-hand front seat and flings

16

himself onto it, jamming his heels against the panel behind the destination indicator.

The view ahead has changed. Buildings which at first he takes for disused offices, their windows broken and their exteriors darkened by age, mirror one another across the road. They're warehouses illuminated by increasingly less frequent streetlamps. Black water glints beyonds gaps to his right, while to his left, up slopes no wider than the bus, he glimpses unlit houses crammed together on both sides of alleys which appear to narrow as they climb. He'll make for any second-hand bookshop he sees which is open. Surely he won't be turned off the bus before it brings him to the shops.

When the bus slows, he presses his feet harder against the yielding metal. Two men are standing under an extensively annotated concrete shelter at the corner of an alley, and the foremost of them has extended a white stick like an antenna sensing the approach of the vehicle. The bus screeches to a halt, and Mottershead hears the door flutter open and the stick begin to tap upstairs.

He's assuming that the driver will tone down his driving, but the vehicle jerks forward like a greyhound out of a trap. He's preparing to help until he hears the man's companion following him upstairs. He watches their reflections on the glass in front of him as the man with the stick fumbles for the seat nearest the stairs and lowers himself onto it. Mottershead is shocked to see the companion mimic these actions, all the more so when he realizes why he is acting that way. Both men are blind.

If they don't leave the bus before Mottershead does they'll know that he didn't offer to help. The vehicle slows again, and he's afraid that the driver is about to summon him. No, someone is flagging the bus down, a man craning into the road from beside the stump of a bus-stop.

The door flaps shut, the bus lurches off between the warehouses. The new passenger takes some time to ascend the stairs. At the top he stands gripping the handrail, hunching his shoulders and turning his head tortoise-like. 'Who's here?' he demands.

He's blind too. Mottershead is fighting a guilty compulsion to answer him when the man with the stick says, 'It's us.'

17

'Thought so. Nobody with all their senses is out this early.'

He stumbles across the aisle and placing a hand on each man's scalp to support himself, sits down behind them. It doesn't matter to the three how dark it is, Mottershead reflects, and wonders what job they have been doing. What job has he retired from? Before he can start to remember, the thin voice of the newcomer distracts him. 'Has he seen to the electricity?'

'Not him,' says the man with the stick. 'Too busy thinking of himself.'

'Can't spare a thought for his people,' his companion adds.

'You'd think he'd attend when they try to let him know his lights are going to fail.'

'We'll have some fun when they're out.'

'He'll be sorry he needs his eyes.'

By now Mottershead's embarrassment has been supplanted by nervousness. Surely they wouldn't say such things if they knew they were being overheard. He peers along the passing alleys in the hope that he may see a better reason than his nerves to quit the bus. 'I remember when the lights fused and I got my own back on my dad,' the man with the stick laughs, just as Mottershead catches sight of a lit area beyond two consecutive alleys, which looks like the beginning of a wide street lined with shops. If he has to wait for any bookshops there to open, that's decidedly preferable to skulking in his seat. He plants his feet on the ridged floor and grasping the back of the seat, steers himself into the aisle.

The vehicle provides no means of communicating with the driver. Mottershead could shout or walk noisily, but he doesn't want to startle the three men. He tiptoes to the stairs and is stepping down carefully when the three turn their pale smooth faces to him. All their eyelids are closed, and so flat there might be no eyes behind them. As he falters on the stairs, the trio bursts out laughing.

They've been aware of him all the time. Enraged and bewildered, he clatters downstairs, shouting, 'Hold on!'

The driver brakes as Mottershead gains the lower deck, and Mottershead has to grab the only handhold within reach

– the shoulder of the man in the dark suit. 'What's the upheaval?' the driver complains. 'Want to give us all a heart attack?'

'Sorry,' Mottershead says to the passenger, apologizing not only for grabbing him but for discovering his secret. The man's upper arm is unyielding as plastic; he must have an artificial limb. As the bus regains speed Mottershead staggers to the door, seeing the lit area beyond another alley, shouting 'Let me off here.'

'You're nowhere near where you've paid to go.'

'This is where I want,' Mottershead says through his teeth.

'I doubt it.' Perhaps it's his stature, but the driver has begun to resemble a petulant child thwarted in a game. 'You'll get no change,' he says.

'Keep the change if it makes you happy. Just open up, or I will.'

The driver slams the door open, and a wind howls through the bus. Mottershead is trying to prepare himself to accept the apparent challenge when the driver stamps on the brake, almost flinging him off the platform. 'Thank you,' Mottershead says heavily, holding onto the bus as he steps down.

The door flutters like a crippled wing, and he hears the driver announce to the passengers, 'He thinks change makes us happy.' The vehicle roars away, trailing oily fumes. When at last the fumes disperse it's still visible, a miniature toy far down the long straight road beneath the low black sky. Down there, perhaps because of the distance, the buildings look windowless. He watches until the bus vanishes as though the perspective has shrunk it to nothing, then he surveys where it has left him.

The nearest alley appears to lead into a lightless tunnel. He's about to retreat towards the openings beyond which he saw light, but then the streetlamp overhead allows him to guess at the contents of a window several hundred yards up the alley – piles of old books.

He steps between the walls and hears his rucksack scraping brick. As the darkness thickens underfoot, the sides of the warehouses tower over him. Where the alley bends beyond them, the window of the first building manages to collect a trace of the light, dimly exhibiting the books. He struggles along the passage, his rucksack flopping against the walls like a disabled pursuer, to the window.

He's tightening the shoulder-straps of the rucksack and skewing his head in an attempt to decipher the spines of the books when he becomes aware that the window belongs to a house. It could be displaying books for sale, but that seems increasingly unlikely as he begins to distinguish the room beyond the books. It's a bedroom, and although the disorder on the bed consists mostly of blankets, he can just discern a head protruding from them, its bald scalp glimmering. Before he has time to step back the eyes flicker open, and the occupant of the bed rises up like a mask on a pole draped with blankets, emitting a cry which seems to voice Mottershead's own panic.

Why has the tenant of the room stacked books in the window if he doesn't want to draw attention? Perhaps they're meant to conceal him, a rampart to keep out the world. It seems not to matter which way Mottershead runs so long as the figure he's disturbed can't see him. By the time he regains some control of himself, he's out of sight of the main road.

Terraced houses crowd on both sides of him, their blackened curtains merging with the black glass of the windows. A hint of light between two houses entices him onwards. It's leaking from the mouth of an alley which should lead to the shops he glimpsed from the bus. The high uninterrupted walls of the alley bend left several hundred yards in, towards the source of the light. He dodges into the alley, glancing back for fear that whoever he disturbed may have followed him.

He's heartened by the sight which greets him at the bend. Ahead the alley intersects a lane of unlit terraced houses, on the far side of which it runs straight to a distant pavement illuminated by shops. He's crossing the junction when he notices that the right-hand stretch of the narrow lane is scattered with dozens of dilapidated books and sections of books.

This time there's no doubt that he has found a bookshop. The downstairs windows of two adjacent houses give him a view of a huge room full of shelves stuffed with books. There must be a light in the room, though it's too feeble to locate. Apparently the entrance is in the rear wall. He darts into the passage which divides the shop from the neighbouring houses, and the walls tug at his rucksack as if someone is trying to pull him back.

The passage leads him not to a street but to a back alley alongside the yards of the houses. He has to sidle between the walls to reach the alley he was previously following. There must be a dog in the yard shared by the houses which comprise the bookshop; he hears its claws scrabbling at concrete and scraping the far side of the insecure wall as it leaps repeatedly at him. He can only assume it has lost its voice. A protrusion on the gate of the yard catches a strap of his rucksack, and he almost tears the fabric in his haste to free himself.

At the alley he turns left, determined to find the entrance to the bookshop. As he reaches the junction he grunts with surprise. The glow from the shop has brightened, illuminating the lane, which has been cleared of books. The doorway between the windows is bricked up, but the glow outlines the glass panel of a door to their left. The panel bears an OPEN sign, and the door is ajar.

Since there's no sign of a proprietor or even of a desk where one might sit, Mottershead calls 'Hello' as he crosses the threshold. Only an echo of his voice responds, and is immediately suppressed by tons of stale paper, but the presence of so many books is enough of a response. They occupy all four walls to the height of the ceiling, and half a dozen double-sided bookcases extend almost the length of the shop, presenting their ends to him. There's barely room for him to sidle between the volumes which protrude into the dim aisles. Shrugging off his rucksack, he lets it fall beside the door.

He's becoming an expert, he thinks. One glance enables him to locate titles he has seen in every second-hand bookshop he has visited so far: *Closeup, The Riverside Villas Murder, The Birds Fall Down*, sets of the works of Dickens, dozens of issues of the *National Geographic*, editions of Poe. The material which appeals to him will be further from the entrance – books by countless forgotten authors whose work

21

he can enjoy reviving for himself while he sits and waits for customers in his own shop. The notion that although these authors are either dead or as good as dead, he can choose to resurrect whatever they achieved as the fancy guides him, makes him feel as if he has found within himself a power he wasn't aware of possessing.

He's pacing along the line of bookcases in order to decide which aisle looks most promising when the spines of a set of volumes beyond them, on the highest of the shelves on the back wall, catch his eye. The fat spines, patterned like old bark and embossed with golden foliage, appear to be emitting the glow which lights the shop; presumably its source is concealed by the bookcases. Without having read the titles, he knows he wants the trinity of books. Since they're too hefty for even his rucksack to bear, he'll arrange to have them sent once he finds the proprietor.

He doesn't immediately notice that he's hesitating. What did he glimpse as he moved away from the door? He turns to squint at the shelves he initially dismissed, which contain the books whose titles he wouldn't have been able to discern in the gloom if they weren't already so familiar. He sees the book at once, and has the disconcerting impression that its neighbours have rearranged themselves, the better to direct his attention to it. He doesn't understand why the nondescript grubby spine should have any significance for him. Hooking one finger in the stall which the top of the spine has become, he drags the book off the shelf.

The illustration on the rubbed cover depicts a man's face composed of a host of unlikely objects. He hasn't time to examine it in detail, even though the face is familiar, because the words seem to leap at him. The title of the novel is *Cadenza*, and the author's name is Simon Mottershead.

He's able to believe it's only a coincidence until he opens the back cover. Though the photograph may be years or even decades younger than he is, the face which gazes up at him from the flap of the jacket is unquestionably the face he saw in the bathroom mirror.

He slams the cover as if he's crushing a spider. His mind feels dark and crowded; he knows at once that he has forgotten more than the book. He's tempted to replace it on the shelf and run out of the shop, but he mustn't give way to panic. 'Is there anyone here but me?' he shouts.

This time not even the echo responds, though someone must previously have unlocked the door and picked up the books in the lane. Perhaps they're upstairs, but he wonders suddenly if the bookseller may be the person he disturbed by staring into the bedroom. On the whole he thinks he would rather not meet the proprietor face to face. He'll pay for the book in his hand and leave a note asking for the others to be reserved for him until a price has been agreed. He's relieved to see a credit card machine and a dusty sheaf of vouchers on a shelf to the left of the door. He gropes in his pocket for his credit card and a scrap of paper.

There's a solitary folded sheet. He shoves the book into the rucksack and unfolds the page. Two-thirds of it is covered with notes for a lecture. At the top, surrounded by a web of doodling, he has written the word LIBRARY and a date. 'Today,' he gasps.

He's supposed to be lecturing to a writer's group. His mind feels as if it's bursting out of his skull. He digs his nails into his scalp, trying to hold onto his memory until he has recaptured all of it, but he can remember nothing else: neither the name nor the whereabouts of the library, not the name of whoever invited him nor of the group itself. Worst of all, he can't recall what time he has undertaken to be there. He's sure he will be late.

He grabs a pencil from beside the credit card machine. Flattening the page against the end of a bookcase, he prints the shortest message he can think of: PLEASE COMMUNICATE WITH ME RE THESE. He adds his details and then squirms along the nearest aisle, tearing off the message as he goes. Floorboards sag, books quiver around him and above him; he's afraid the bookcases will fall and bury him. By craning towards the tomes he's just able to insert the slip of paper into the niche formed by the florid cornice and the top of the leafy oaken binding. He leaves it dangling, a tongue blackened by his name, and retreats towards the door.

He still has to buy his own book. He pins a voucher with finger and thumb against the door, which shakes with every movement of the pencil as though someone crouching out of sight is attempting to fumble it open. A mixture of embarrassment at the small amount and determination to see his name clear makes him press so hard with the pencil that the voucher tears as he signs it, and the plumbago breaks. He lays the voucher in the metal bed and inserts his card in the recess provided, then he drags the handle over them to emboss the voucher. As the handle passes over his card there's a sound like teeth grinding, and he feels the card break.

He wrenches the slide back to its starting point and gapes at the card, which has snapped diagonally in half. He opens his mouth to yell for the proprietor, having forgotten his nervousness, but then he sees that the lead which broke off the pencil was under the card when he used the embosser. Shoving his copy of the voucher into his pocket together with the pointed blades which are the halves of the card, he pokes his arms through the straps of the rucksack and flounces out, his book bumping his spine as if it's trying to climb the bony ladder and reinsert its tale into his brain.

The street is grey with a twilight which appears to seep out of the bricks and the pavement, much as mist seems to rise from the ground. A few windows are lit, but no curtains are open. He runs to the junction of the lane and the alley and listens for traffic. The only noises are the slam of an opened door and a rush of feet which sound as though they're stumbling over parts of themselves. Even if they're wearing slippers too large for them, their approach is enough to send Mottershead fleeing towards the light which was his original destination – fleeing so hastily that his impression of his destination doesn't change until he is almost there.

The area is floodlit, though several of the floodlights have been overturned on the flagstones with which the street is paved. Broken saplings strapped to poles loll in concrete tubs along the centre of the street. All the shops are incomplete, but he can't tell whether they are being built or demolished. The figures which peer over the exposed girders and fragments of walls aren't workmen; they're plastic mannequins, more convincingly flesh-coloured than is usually the case. Vandals must have had some fun with them, because they are all beckoning to Mottershead, or are they gesturing him onwards? Their eyes are unpleasantly red. As he blinks at the nearest, he sees that someone has painstakingly added crimson veins to the painted eyeballs. A wind from the bay flaps the plastic sheets which have been substituted for roofs, the crippled saplings creak as their elongated shadows grope over the flagstones, and beneath the flapping he thinks he hears the creak of plastic limbs.

To his left the paved area curves out of sight towards the bay. To his right, perhaps half a mile distant, several cars are parked. Mustn't they be on or near a road? Willing the cars to be taxis, he sprints towards them.

The roofs stir as if the skeletons of buildings are trying to awaken. Whenever they do so, the arms of the mannequins wave stiffly at him. The state of the figures grows worse as he progresses: some are handless, and brandish rusty prongs protruding from their wrists; most are bald, and those which aren't wear their wigs askew – one wig as grey as matted dust has slipped down to cover a face. All the figures are naked, and sport unlikely combinations of genitalia, presumably thanks to vandalism. Some of the heads have been turned completely round on the necks, which are mottled as senile flesh. As he passes one such figure it falls forward, rattling the bars of the stranded lift which cages it, and Mottershead claps a hand to his chest as he runs onwards.

By now he can see that each of the three cars is occupied, but suppose a car dealer has propped mannequins in each of the drivers' seats? The roofs writhe, and a bald figure sprawls towards him, leaving behind the hand with which it was supporting itself on the back of a solitary dining-chair. Its head is hollow, and empty now that the contents have scuttled away behind a girder. He would cry out if he had breath to do so, but surely there's no need, since the three figures in the cars have sat up and turned towards him. He's no longer alone with the tread, floppy but not quite barefoot, which is following him. He lunges for the foremost vehicle, his eyes so blurred with exertion that he can hardly see the door. He's near to panic before his fingertips snag the handle. He levers it up and collapsing into the back seat, slams the door.

However much of a relief it is just to sit there with his eyes closed, he has to keep moving. 'The library,' he wheezes.

Either the driver is taciturn by nature or he's losing his voice. 'Which?'

At least he seems unlikely to trouble Mottershead with the unnecessary chatter typical of his species, but his response sounds suspiciously like an imitation of Mottershead's wheezing. 'The one where a writers' group meets,' Mottershead says, interrupting himself twice as he tries to catch his breath.

He's hoping that his words will provoke a further question which may help him clarify his thoughts. To his surprise, the driver starts the car, and Mottershead lets himself sink into the seat, feeling sponge swell to meet his hands through the torn upholstery. When he's no longer aware of having to make himself breathe, he looks where he's going.

The incomplete buildings have been left behind. The car is passing a concrete edifice guarded by railings like fossilized branches and twigs. Despite the stained glass in its windows and the inscriptions carved in scrolls over its broad doorways, it must be a factory rather than a church. Coaches whose windows are impenetrably black are parked inside the gates, and thousands of people, all of them carrying objects which may be toolkits or briefcases and wearing brightly coloured overalls in which they resemble overgrown toddlers, are marching silently into the building. He's trying to decipher the writing on the carved scrolls when he notices that the driver is watching him.

As soon as Mottershead's gaze meets his, the man fixes his attention on the road. Mottershead is almost certain that he is wearing a wig, a curly red wig twice as wide as his neck, above which it perches like a parasite which has drained all colour from the rings of pudgy flesh. The mirror seems to have lent the reflection of his eyes some of its glassiness, for although they're bloodshot, they look dollish – indeed, a flaw in the mirror makes the left eye appear to have been turned inside out. Mottershead throws himself about on the seat in order to shed the rucksack and reach his book.

He intends it both to help him ignore the driver and to revive his ideas for the lecture, but as soon as he reads the opening sentence – 'He knows this dark' – he feels threatened by remembering too much. He skims the long paragraphs packed with detail as the unnamed protagonist listens to the dawn chorus and lets his other senses feast on his surroundings, which sunlight and his awareness of his own mortality are beginning to renew. Mottershead has glanced at only the first few pages when the memory of labouring on the novel begins to form like a charred coal in his mind. He leafs back towards the dedication, but slams the book shut as he realizes that the taxi is drawing up at the kerb.

He stuffs the book into the rucksack and stares about him. He's outside the entrance to a shopping mall, a pair of glass doors framed by several neon tubes whose glare is almost blinding. 'I want the library,' he protests.

'You've got it.'

There's no doubt now that the driver is mimicking him, raising the pitch of his voice as Mottershead did. 'I can't see it,' Mottershead says furiously.

'You will.'

Mottershead imagines his own voice being forced to rise as the argument continues, topping the driver's mimicry until it becomes a screech. He flings himself out of the vehicle, almost tripping over the rucksack, and thumps the door shut with his buttocks. 'What are you expecting?'

'Two and a big pointed one.'

Mottershead produces the twenty-pound note. He wishes he could see the driver's face, but the neon at the entrance to the mall has dazzled him. 'I've nothing else to offer you.'

'You delight me,' says the driver in exactly the same tone. He takes the note and hands Mottershead a smaller one. Mottershead keeps his hand extended, though he isn't looking forward to a repetition of the driver's touch; the man's stubby fingertips seem to lack nails. He's still awaiting change when he hears the driver release the handbrake, and the taxi speeds away.

'Wait,' Mottershead neighs, struggling to see past the blur which coats his eyes. He slaps his empty hand over his face and stands crying 'Stop thief.' The noise of the vehicle fades more swiftly than the blur, until he begins to plead for his sight. Nothing matters more than being able to see. He'll let the driver go if he can only have his vision back.

At last his sight clears. He's beside a dual carriageway, across which the long blank slab of the shopping mall faces acres of waste ground where a few starved shrubs are decorated with litter. Above the carriageway, red lamps grow pale as the light of a glassy sun glares across the waste. There's no sign of the taxi among the traffic which races along both sides of the road, turning grey with the dust in the air. 'Good riddance,' Mottershead mumbles, and glances at the note in his hand. It's his own twenty-pound note, except that part of it – about an eighth – has been torn off.

He emits a shriek of rage and swivels wildly. His movement prompts the doors of the mall to slide open, and he veers towards them, through an arch of massive concrete blocks reminiscent of the entrance to an ancient tomb. As soon as he has passed between the doors they whisper shut behind him.

The mall is three floors high. Shops and boarded-up rooms surround a wide tiled area on which more than a dozen concrete drums containing flowers and shrubs are arranged in a pattern he can't quite identify. The air is full of a thin sound, either piped music or the twittering of the birds which are flying back and forth under the glassed-in girders of the roof. Escalators rise from the centre of the open space, bearing figures so stiffly posed that they look unreal. He barely notices all this as he dashes into the nearest shop.

It's a video library called Sammy's Hat. Cracked plastic spines are crammed into shelves on the walls which flank the counter, behind which a large man is watching a dwarfish television. IF YOU'RE NOT HAPPY WITH OUR SERVICE is printed on the front of his T-shirt, which is close to strangling his thick arms and neck beneath his raddled sprawling face. Cassette boxes flaunt their covers behind him: *Don't Look in the Oven*, *The Puncturer*, *Rude and Naked*, *Out of His Head*. . . . He acknowledges Mottershead only by ducking closer to the television, which is receiving the credits of a film called *Nasty, Brutish and Short*. 'Is it possible for me to phone?' Mottershead says over the buzzing of kazoos.

28

The shopman's small eyes narrow. 'Anything's possible here.'

'I mean, may I use your phone?'

The man heaves a sigh which sets boxes rattling on the shelves. 'What's it all about?'

'I've been robbed,' Mottershead declares, waving the remains of the note. 'I just paid my taxi fare with this, and this is what the cabby gave me back.'

On the tiny screen a stooge who appears to be wearing a monkish wig is poking two fingers in another's eyes. The shopman throws himself back in his high chair, chortling so grossly that his saliva sizzles on the screen. 'Come and see this,' he shouts.

A woman tented from neck to feet in gingham squeezes through a doorway behind him. Her ruddy face is even wider than his, her eyes smaller. Mottershead assumes that the shopman has called her to watch the film until the man points at the torn note. 'That's what he got when he tried to pay his fare with it,' he splutters.

Mottershead feels another screech of rage building up inside him, but it will only waste time; he won't be penniless for long – he'll be paid for the lecture. 'Forget it,' he says when the hoots and howls of the couple squashed behind the counter begin to relent. 'Just tell me where the library is.'

The woman lifts her dress, revealing thighs like a pink elephant's, to wipe her eyes. 'You're in it, you poor bat.'

'Not this kind. The kind with books.'

Mottershead intends his tone to be neutral, but the shopman flings himself like a side of beef across the counter and makes a grab for his lapels. 'You watch what you're saying to my daughter. Nothing in here to be ashamed of. Stories, that's all they are.'

Mottershead backs out of reach, his ankles scraping together. 'You don't deserve to have eyes if that's the best you can do with them,' he says from the door.

He's hoping to seek help from a security guard, but none is to be seen. At least the couple aren't following him; they've begun to pummel each other, whether because they are choking with laughter or for some more obscure purpose he can't tell. He dodges into the next shop, a tobacconist's full of smoke. 'Can you tell me where the library is?'

'At the end.'

Perhaps the tobacconist is distracted, having apparently just singed his eyebrows while tuning the flame of a lighter. When Mottershead runs to the far end of the mall he finds only a baker's. 'Library?' he wheezes.

'Who says?' The baker looks ready to turn worse than unhelpful. He's digging his fingers into a skull-sized lump of dough which has already been shaped; a swarm of raisins oozes from the sockets into which he has thrust his thumbs. 'Thanks anyway,' Mottershead blurts, and retreats.

One of the assistants in the adjacent toy shop leaves off playing long enough to direct him. 'Up and through,' he says, and points a dripping water pistol at him.

Mottershead is afraid that the gun may fire and ruin his lecture notes, and so he makes for the escalators as the assistants recommence chasing one another through the chaos of toys, which reminds him more of a playroom than of a shop. The extravagant threats they're issuing in falsetto voices fade as the deserted stairs lift him towards the roof.

Like the vegetation in the concrete tubs, on closer examination the birds beneath the roof prove to be artificial. Several birds are pursuing their repetitive flights upside down, presumably because of some fault in the mechanism, and their maker appears not to have thought it necessary to provide any of them with eyes. Mottershead finds the spectacle so disagreeably fascinating that he's almost at the top before he notices that someone has stepped forward to meet him.

She's a woman in her sixties whose hair is dyed precisely the same shade of pale blue as her coat. Her flat chest sports a tray which contains a collecting-tin and a mound of copies of the badge pinned to her lapel. 'Is there a library here, do you know?' he pleads.

The woman stares at him. Perhaps she didn't hear him for the mechanical twittering of the birds. The escalator raises him until he's a head taller than she is, and he repeats the question. This time she lifts the tin from its nest of badges, which say PENSIONERS IN PERIL in letters red as blood, and rattles it at him. 'I'm sorry, I've no money,' he complains.

Of course, her stare has grown accusing because he's still holding the remains of the twenty-pound note. 'This won't be any use to you. Can't you tell me where the library is?'

Her only response is a look of contempt, and he loses his temper. 'Take it if you've got a use for it,' he shouts, 'if it'll persuade you to answer a simple question.'

As he begins to shout, a security guard emerges from a greetings-card shop and jogs towards them. 'Is he bothering you?' the guard demands.

'I just want the library,' Mottershead wails, seeing himself as the guard must see him, towering over the pensioner and yelling at her. Worse, she has taken the torn note from him, and now she has found her voice. 'He tried to pass me this.'

'Because you insisted,' Mottershead protests, but the guard examines the note before he turns on Mottershead, frowning through the shadow of his peaked cap. 'I'd say you owe this lady more than an apology.'

'I tried to tell her I've no money.' Receiving only stares from both of them, Mottershead blunders on: 'I'm a writer. I'm needed at the library. They've asked me to talk.'

'So have we,' the guard says ponderously. Then the woman stuffs the note into her tin and waves Mottershead away as if he's an insect she can't be bothered to swat, and the guard grasps his shoulder. 'Let's make sure you end up where you're wanted.'

Before Mottershead quite knows what's happening, he is being marched to the end of the mall above the baker's. Here, invisible from below, is an unmarked door. When the guard leans on a bellpush beside it Mottershead starts to panic, especially when the door is opened by another man in uniform. He can't judge how large the cell beyond the door may be; it's piled with cartons, and the passage between them is scarcely two men wide. The guard who is holding him tells the other, 'He claims you've invited him to talk.'

'Show him through, love. He'll be for the soundproof room.'

He flattens himself against the cartons to make way, and the guard pats his plump buttocks with one hand as he shoves Mottershead into the passage. The uniformed man purrs like a big cat and rubs himself against the cartons. 'Hold on,' Mottershead protests, 'where are you taking—' Then the guard reaches past him and opens a door, and Mottershead's voice booms out beyond it, earning him so many disapproving stares that he would retreat into the cell if it weren't for the guard.

He's reached his destination by a back door. The library is as large as the mall, and disconcertingly similar, except that the walls which overlook the escalators are occupied by books rather than by shops. In front of the multitude of books are more tables for readers than he's able to count, and all the readers are glaring at him. 'Where am I meant to go?' he mutters.

'I'll walk you,' the guard says, and steers him leftwards. 'What was the name?'

'Simon Mottershead.' He raises his voice in the hope that some of the readers will recognize his name, but they only look hostile. He lets himself be ushered past the tables, trying to think how to convince the readers that he isn't a miscreant. He hasn't succeeded in dredging up a single thought when the guard marshals him left again, through a doorway between shelves of Bibles and other religious tomes, into a room.

The room is white and windowless. Several ranks of seats composed of plastic slabs and metal tubing face away from the door, towards a single chair behind a table bearing a carafe and a glass. About twenty people are scattered among the seats, mostly near the table. Before Mottershead can make for it, the guard leans on his shoulder and sits him in the seat nearest the door. 'Simon Mottershead,' the guard announces.

Every head glances back and then away. 'Not here,' someone says.

The guard's hand shifts ominously on Mottershead's shoulder. 'I'm Simon Mottershead,' Mottershead stammers. 'Isn't this the writers' group?'

This time only a few heads respond, and someone murmurs 'Who?' Eventually a woman rumbles, 'Are we expected to turn our seats to you?'

'Not if I'm allowed to move.' Mottershead heaves himself to his feet and shrugging off the guard's grasp, turns to stare him away. The man's expression is so disappointed and wistful that it throws him, and he blunders towards the table, struggling to unstrap his rucksack.

He hears the guard trudge out and close the door, though not before admitting someone else. The latecomer is wearing either slippers or sandals. The sound of footsteps flopping after him makes Mottershead feel pursued, and unwilling to look back. By the time he's past the table, the newcomer is already seated. Mottershead drags the chair out from the table and dumps his rucksack on the floor, seats himself, lifts the inverted glass from the carafe and turns it over. When nobody comes forward to introduce him, he looks up.

He can't identify the latecomer. He doesn't think it would be any of the several elderly women who sit clutching handbags or manuscripts, more than one of which is protected by a knitted cover. It might be one of the young women who are staring hard at him and poising pencils over notepads, or it could be one of the men – not those who resemble army officers, red-faced with suppressing thoughts, but possibly the lanky man who reminds Mottershead of a horse propped on its tailbone, his shoulders almost level with his ears as he grips his knees and crouches low in his seat, or the man whose bald head gleams behind a clump of hatted women. Every eye is on Mottershead, aggravating his awareness that he's meant to speak. He tips the carafe and discovers that it contains not water but a film of dust. 'As I say, I'm Simon Mottershead,' he says, fumbling for his notes.

His audience looks apathetic, perhaps because they're wondering why he is digging in his pockets with both hands. He must have dropped his notes in the bookshop; his pockets are empty except for the voucher and the pieces of his credit card. 'What would you like me to talk about?' he says desperately.

The faces before him turn blank as if their power has been switched off. 'Tell us about yourself,' says a voice he's unable to locate or to sex.

He feels trapped by the question, bereft of words. 'Are you married with children?' the voice says.

'Not any more.'

'Did it help your writing?'

At least Mottershead has answers, even if they're almost too quick for him. 'Nobody except a writer knows how it feels to be a writer.'

'Harrumph har*rumph* humph,' a red-faced man on the front row responds.

'I'll tell you how it felt to me,' Mottershead says more sharply. 'Every day I'd be wakened by a story aching to be told. Writing's a compulsion. By the time you're any good at it you no longer have the choice of giving it up. It won't leave you alone even when you're with people, even when you're desperate to sleep.'

By now the faces are so expressionless that he can imagine them fading like masks moulded out of dough. 'When it comes to life,' he says, anxious to raise his own spirits as much as those of his audience, 'it's like seeing everything with new eyes. It's like dreaming while you're awake. It's as if your mind's a spider which is trying to catch reality and spin it into patterns.'

'Harrumph harrumph harrumph,' the red-faced man enunciates slowly, and leaves it at that. As Mottershead ransacks his mind for memories which don't cause it to flinch, the voice which raised the question of his family speaks. 'What's it like to be published?'

'Not as different from not being as you'd think. I used to say I expected the priest at my funeral to ask, "Did he write under his own name?" and, "Should I have heard of him?" and, "How many novels did he write a year?"'

He's hoping to provoke at least a titter, but no face stirs. 'Weren't you on television?' says the voice, which is coming from the bald head beyond the hats.

'Exactly,' Mottershead laughs. Then the questioner sidles into view, and Mottershead sees that he wasn't suggesting another cliché but trying to remind him. 'If you say so,' Mottershead says unevenly. 'I told a story once about someone who thought he was.'

He's closer than ever to panic, and the sight of his questioner doesn't help. He assumes it's a man, even though the appearance of baldness proves to have been achieved by a flesh-coloured hairnet or skullcap. Although nearly all the flesh of his long mottled face has settled into his

34

jowls, this person isn't as thin as he seemed to be when only his scalp was visible; it's as if he somehow rendered himself as presentable as possible before letting Mottershead see him. His large dark eyes glisten like bubbles about to pop, and his unwavering gaze makes Mottershead feel in danger of being compelled to speak before he knows what he will say. 'Everything's material, anything can start a story growing in your head. Maybe that's our compensation for having to use up so much of ourselves in writing that nobody wants to know us.'

The man with the unconvincing scalp looks suspicious and secretly gleeful. When his piebald mouth opens, Mottershead stiffens, though the question sounds innocent enough. 'Do you still write?'

'I'm leaving it to people like yourselves.'

If that signifies anything beyond allowing Mottershead to feel relatively in control, it ought to encourage the audience, but the questioner smiles as if Mottershead has betrayed himself. The smile causes the upper set of the teeth he's wearing to drop, revealing gums black as a dog's, and he sticks out his tongue to lever the teeth into place. 'Wouldn't they give you a chance?'

'Who?'

'The powers that decide what people can read.'

Everyone nods in agreement. 'I don't think we need to look for conspiracies,' Mottershead says, feeling as if his own teeth are exposed.

'Then why did you stop?'

He means stop writing, Mottershead assures himself. The man's gaze is a spotlight penetrating the secret places of his brain. 'Because it wasn't worth it. It wasn't worth my expending so much of myself on creating the absolute best I was capable of when nobody cared that I had.'

'Don't you think you were lucky to be published at all?'

The man's whitish tongue is ranging about his lips; he's begun to look as mentally unstable as Mottershead suspects he is. Genius may be next to madness, Mottershead thinks, but so is mediocrity and worse where creativity is concerned. 'I think that's up to my readers to judge, don't you? What does anyone who's read my books think?'

He lets his attention drift heavenwards, or at least towards the twiglike cracks and peeling leaves of plaster which compose the ceiling. When his pretence of indifference produces no response, he sneaks a glance at his audience. How can the back of every head be facing him? 'Anyone who's read anything,' he says, attempting a careless laugh. 'Someone must have read me or I wouldn't be here.'

The pink-scalped man rears up, knotting the belt of his faded and discoloured overcoat which could almost be a dressing-gown. 'Remind us,' he says.

At least the audience is watching Mottershead, but without warmth. 'I expect you'll have heard of *Cadenza*. That was my best book.'

'Who says?' his interrogator demands.

'I do.' There must have been reviews, and surely Mottershead had friends who gave him their opinions, but where those memories should be is only darkness. 'I put everything I could into that book, everything of myself that was worth having. It's about the last days of a man who knows he's dying, and how that gives new life to everything we take for granted.'

'How does it end?'

'I'll tell you,' Mottershead says, only to discover that the dark has swallowed that information too. 'Or perhaps,' he corrects himself hastily, 'someone who's read it should.'

The doughy faces slump. Nobody has read the book. The bald man's stare is probing his thoughts, and he feels as if he's being asked, 'Why do you write?' – being compelled to answer, 'Life is shit and that's why I use up so much paper.' He's opening his mouth – anything to break the breathless silence – when it occurs to him that he needn't try to recall the end of the book. He grabs the rucksack and placing it on the table in front of him, unfastens the buckles and opens it towards his audience like a stage magician, displaying the book. 'This is me.'

It's immediately obvious that he has blundered somehow. 'I beg your pardon. This is I,' he says, and when their expressions grow more unconvinced: 'This am I? I am this?'

The bald man smirks. 'I should let it drop.'

They needn't quiz Mottershead's grammar; some of them are bound to have perpetrated worse. Losing patience, he lifts the book out of the rucksack, and sees why they are unimpressed. His name is no longer on the cover.

He must have torn the jacket as he shoved the book into the rucksack; it's missing from the front of the book and from the spine, the binding of which is blank. He pulls the rucksack open wide, then forces it inside out, but nothing falls from it except a scattering of soil.

'Har-rumph,' the red-faced man pronounces, and several heads nod vigorously. The man with the pink scalp, whose cap fits so snugly that it seems to be flattening flesh as well as any hair which the headgear conceals, stares wide-eyed at Mottershead. By God, he'll show them he wrote the novel. He throws it open, its cover striking the table with a sound like a lid being cast off a box, and finds that the copyright and title pages have been torn out. There's no trace of his name in the book.

He can still display the photograph inside the back cover, which seems impatient to be opened; he's almost sure that he feels the book stir. He picks it up gingerly, but the table beneath it is bare. He squeezes the volume between his hands and lets it fall open.

Perhaps his face is on the flap, but so is an object which has been squashed between the cover and the flyleaf. It's where he remembers the photograph to have been, and the markings on its back are very like a face. Despite its having been flattened, it retains some life. He has barely glimpsed it when it raises itself and staggering rapidly off the book, drops into his lap.

He screams and leaps to his feet, hurling the book away from him. The object, whose welter of legs makes it appear to have doubled in size, falls to the floor and scuttles through a crack beneath the skirting-board. The audience watch as if they're wondering what further antics Mottershead may perform in a vain attempt to shock them into responding. 'I'll show you,' he babbles. 'Just talk among yourselves while I fetch a book.'

Everyone turns to watch him as he heads for the door, forcing himself to walk as though he doesn't feel like running out of the room. Nobody speaks while he struggles with the mechanism of the door, twisting a knob above the handle back and forth until he hears a click and the door swings open. He steps out and pulls it to behind him.

Either the readers at the tables are engrossed in their work or they're consciously ignoring him. He tries to move quietly as he hurries from shelf to shelf. Once he identifies the fiction, surely he'll find one or more of his books. All the shelves on this side of the top floor, however, hold only books about psychology and religion, arranged according to some system he can't crack. He sidles between two tables, ensuring that he doesn't brush against the Bible readers in front of him, and his buttocks bump a woman's head. She's wearing a rain hat which resembles a shower cap, and it must be this which deflates at the contact, but it feels as if her skull has yielded like a dying balloon, a sensation so disconcerting that the apology he means to offer comes out as 'My pleasure.' Feeling at the mercy of his own words, he blunders to the edge of the balcony and clutches the handrail.

If the fiction is shelved separately from the rest of the stock, he can't see where; every visible shelf holds books larger than any novel, some as thick and knobbly as full-grown branches. As he runs on tiptoe to the down escalator, a sprint which takes him halfway around the perimeter, a few readers glower at him. They would be better employed, he thinks, in complaining about the muffled shouts and thumping, presumably of workmen, which have begun somewhere offstage. A stair crawls out of hiding and catches his heel with a clang that reverberates through the library, and he sails down to the counter.

This is shaped like a symbol of hope, a curve stretching out its arms towards a way of escape. Two librarians with wide flat faces sit shoulder to shoulder at a table behind it, poring over a tome Mottershead takes to be an encyclopaedia of wild animals. He shuffles his feet, clears his throat, knocks on the counter. 'Hello?' he pleads.

One librarian removes her steel-framed spectacles and passes them to her colleague, who uses them to peer more closely at an illustration. 'Better see what the row is,' he suggests.

Mottershead is framing a tart response when he realizes that even now they aren't acknowledging him. Both raise their heads towards the shouts and pounding on the top floor. They could be identical twins, and their stubbly scalps, together with the pinstripe suits and shirts and ties they're wearing, seem designed to confuse him. 'Can you tell me where to find your fiction?' he says urgently.

'You'll see none of that here,' the man says without a glance at him.

'What, nowhere in the library?'

'Only books about it,' says the woman, watching someone moving behind and above him.

'No need for fiction here.' The man returns her spectacles to her and nods at the book on the desk. It isn't about animals, Mottershead sees now; it's a study of deformed babies, open at a picture of one which appears to have been turned inside out at birth. He's glad to be distracted by a commotion on the top floor, a door releasing a stampede of footsteps and a protesting hubbub – glad, that is, until he looks up.

The uniformed man who admitted him has let the writers out of the room, which is indeed almost soundproof. They glare about the balcony, ignoring the shushing and tutting of the readers, and then several women brandishing handbags and manuscripts catch sight of Mottershead. They rush to the edge and point at him, crying 'He locked us in.'

'I didn't mean to,' Mottershead calls, but the entire library responds with a sound like the dousing of a great fire. 'I didn't mean to,' he confides to the librarians, who shrug in unison as the writers march away along the balcony. 'Where are they going?'

'Where they came from, I expect,' the male librarian says with satisfaction.

'But I haven't finished!' Mottershead flaps his arms, and is preparing to shout when the stares of all the readers gag him. Perhaps he should let the writers go, especially since he hasn't found a book to show them – but then he realizes what he has forgotten. 'I haven't been paid.'

The female librarian tosses her head to prevent her spectacles from slipping off her rudimentary nose. 'No use telling us.'

'Don't you know who's in charge?' Mottershead begs.

'You want his holiness.'

'The reverend,' her colleague explains.

He's pointing at the red-faced man whose entire vocabulary seemed to consist of false coughs, and who is making his way around the balcony towards the down escalator. Mottershead pads to the foot of the escalator, trying to phrase a demand which will be polite but firm. 'I believe I'm to be paid now,' he rehearses as the red-faced man comes abreast of the escalator. The man marches past without sparing it or Mottershead a glance.

Is there another public exit besides the one beyond the counter? Mottershead groans aloud and sprints to the opposite escalator, dodging irate readers who twist in their seats and try to detain him. He grabs the banister, which squirms as it slithers upwards, and runs up the lumbering stairs.

As soon as he's three stairs short of the balcony he manages to heave himself onto it, using the banisters like parallel bars. The only door he can locate leads to the stockroom through which the guard brought him, but he shouldn't be searching for a door. The red-faced man is returning to the down escalator, having replaced a hymn-book on the shelf.

Mottershead clutches his aching skull. It will take him several minutes to run around the balcony to that escalator, by which time his quarry may well have left the building. 'Reverend,' he calls desperately. 'Reverend! *Reverend!*'

The man seems not to hear him. Either he's experiencing a vision which renders him unaware of his surroundings as he rides towards the ground floor, or his title is only the librarians' nickname for him. Mottershead lurches onto the stairs which are climbing doggedly towards him and clatters down, shouting 'Hey! Hey! Hey!' Even now the red-faced man doesn't look at him, though all the readers do; many of them start to boo and jeer. While Mottershead is managing to outrun the escalator, his quarry is descending at more than twice his speed. He's only halfway down when the red-faced man steps onto the floor and strides past the counter.

'My fee,' Mottershead screams. He lifts his feet and slides down, his heels clanking on the edges of the steps. At the bottom he launches himself between the tables, where at least one reader sticks out a foot for him to jump over. The exit

barrier is executing a last few swings, but the red-faced man is already past the doors beyond it. Mottershead is almost at the counter when the man with the pink scalp steps into his path.

'Let me pass,' Mottershead cries, but the man widens his glistening eyes and stretches out his arms on either side of him. The librarians are miming indifference, gazing at the roof. 'Get away or I'll buffet and belabour you,' Mottershead snarls, which earns him admonitory looks from the librarians. He's poising himself to rush his tormentor when the man steps forward, soles flapping. 'Reverend Neverend said to give you this.'

Is he protracting a joke which the librarians played on Mottershead? But he's waving an envelope, brown as the wrapper of a book which has something to hide. Mottershead suspects that it contains a text he has no desire to read. 'Didn't he even have the grace to serve me with it himself?' Mottershead says for the readers to hear, and snatches the envelope. At once he realizes that it's full of coins and notes.

The writers must have held a collection for him. Feeling exposed and clownish, he slips the envelope into his pocket, which he pats to convince himself that he hasn't dropped the envelope, and wills the readers to forget about him. As he tries to sneak past the counter the messenger detains him, seizing his elbow with jittery fingers whose nails are caked with ink. 'Can I talk to you?'

'You have done.'

'That was for the others. I want to talk about ourselves. We've lots in common, I can tell.'

'Some other time,' Mottershead says insincerely, trying to pull away without looking at him.

'There won't be.'

'So be it, then.' Mottershead attempts to stare him into letting go, but can't meet the other's eyes for long; they look as if being compelled to see too much has swollen them almost too large for their sockets. 'I want to be left alone,' he mutters.

'You know that's not possible.'

Mottershead feels black helplessness closing around his mind. He wants to lash out, to thump the man's scalp, which he's sure is plastic disguised not quite successfully as flesh. What would it sound like? The temptation dismays him. 'Will you have a word with this person?' he says at the top of his voice.

The librarians frown at him. 'What about?' the female says.

'About your dress code, I should think.'

The man with the replaced scalp is wearing slippers on his bony feet, and if his buttonless garment belted with old rope isn't a dressing-gown, it might as well be; certainly he's wearing nothing under it except striped trousers like a sleeper's or a convict's. The librarians are still frowning at Mottershead, but he doesn't care, because his outburst has caused his tormentor to flinch and loosen his spidery grip. He pulls himself free and knees the barrier aside, shouting 'I think you've got some explaining to do' to freeze the man in case he considers following. He closes both hands around the heavy brass knob of the door and having opened it just wide enough to sidle through, drags it shut behind him.

He has emerged onto an avenue lined with shops beneath a heavily overcast sky. Display windows shine between treetrunks as far as the eye can see. Though the upper storeys are obscured by foliage, it seems to him that the shops have taken over a variety of buildings; through the leaves he glimpses creatures so immobile they must be gargoyles, bricked-up towers like trees pruned to the trunk, domes green as mounds of moss. To his right, in the distance where the trees appear to meet, the sky is clear. He heads for the light, hoping it will help him think.

Before long he sees that he's approaching a bookshop, its windows full of paperbacks as bright and various as packets in a supermarket. Wasn't *Cadenza* put into paperback? The thought of the book makes him shriek through his teeth; he has left the damaged copy and his rucksack in the library. He can't imagine going back, but perhaps there is no need. Dodging the bicycles which are the only traffic, he crosses to the bookshop.

The glass doors are plastered with posters for a book called *Princess the Frog*. The sight of eyes bulging at him from beneath crowned bridal veils confuses him, so that he

grapples with the doors for some time before discovering that the right-hand door is locked into position. He shoulders its twin open and thinks he has cracked the glass. No, he has dislodged a poster, which the door crumples and tears. He steps over it and moves quickly into the shop, pretending he was nowhere near.

Fiction is ranged around the walls. Anything by Mottershead ought to be on the shelves at the back of the shop. He's passing the authors beginning with I when someone catches up with him. 'May I help you?'

'I'm looking—' Mottershead begins, and then his voice goes to pieces. He has been accosted by a frog in a wedding dress. In a moment he's able to distinguish that the frog is an elderly woman, her leathery skin painted green with the make-up she has used to make her mouth seem wider. She's holding the poster he crumpled. 'I can find it myself, thank you,' he says in a voice so controlled it feels like stifling a belch.

'Keep in mind that we're here.'

Whether that is meant as a warning or as an offer of assistance, it aggravates the hysteria he's trying to suppress. She has drawn his attention to her colleagues who are scattered about the shop, all of whom, including at least one man, are dressed as bridal frogs. This must be part of a promotion for the book which is advertised on the posters – there's a mound of copies of the book draped with waterweed beside the cash-desk. He clutches his mouth as he begins to splutter, and flees deeper into the shop.

The letter M covers the whole of the back wall. He has the impression that the patterns formed by the print on the spines spell out several giant versions of the letter. His name is almost at floor level – Mottershead, in several different typefaces. He digs his fingers into the tops of the pages and tugs at the four books. No wonder nobody has bought them if they're wedged so tightly on the shelf. He manages to tip them towards himself until he's able to grasp the corners of the spines. He heaves at them, and without warning they fly off the shelf and sprawl across the floor.

Before he can pick them up, the frog bride who originally followed him hurries over. 'It's all right,' Mottershead tells her, feeling his mirth coming to the boil again as he stoops to gather the books. 'I'll buy these if you'll give me a carrier bag. I wrote them.'

Does she think he's lying? Disapproval stretches her mouth wide enough to render her make-up redundant. 'Look,' he says, no longer wanting to laugh, 'I assure you—' Then he sees the covers of the books he's claiming to have written, and his jaw drops.

The author's name is undoubtedly Mottershead; it's spread across the covers in large raised capital letters. The first name, however, is printed small to fit between the thighs of the girls whose naked bottoms are embossed on the covers. The books are called *Eighteen, Seventeen, Sixteen* and *Fifteen*, and it's clear from the faces gazing over their shoulders that these are the ages of the girls. He doesn't need to focus on the author's first name to be certain that he could never have entertained such thoughts, let alone admitting them on paper – but how can he convince the princess frog?

'You'd better have them before I do any more damage,' he mumbles. If she will only take them, he'll run out of the shop; he no longer cares what she thinks of him. But she shakes her head violently and clenches her greenish fists, further crumpling the poster, and two of her fellow frogs close in behind Mottershead. 'Trouble?' the male bride croaks.

'The author of those items claims to have found them on the shelf. One wonders who must have put them there.'

'I was mistaken. I didn't write any of these books.'

The frog with the poster stares incredulously at Mottershead. 'Seems not to know when to stop telling tales,' remarks the fattest of the frogs.

'Do I look as if I could be responsible for this stuff?' Mottershead cries. 'Why would I be trying to buy books I'd written myself?'

The frogs snigger. 'Some people will stop at nothing to promote themselves,' says the one with the poster.

Mottershead is overwhelmed by rage which feels distressingly like panic. He tosses the books into the air and is on his way to the exit before they come down. He's fleeing past the shop when the three booksellers appear at the window, hopping up and down and croaking inarticulately as they wave

46

the books at him. All the passing cyclists begin to ring their bells as if to draw attention to him, and he dodges behind a chestnut tree, turning up his collar to hide the parts of his face he can't squash against the trunk.

As soon as the bellringing slackens he dodges out from behind the tree and hastens along the avenue, trying to outrun a sound which he has begun to suspect is concealed by the jangle of bells. He has passed only a few buildings, however, when he comes to a bookshop which has taken over a cinema. The compulsion to find himself on the shelves is stronger than ever. Glancing along the deserted pavement, he darts into the shop.

Several life-size cut-out figures, presumably of authors rather than of film stars, loiter inside the entrance. Shelves like exposed girders branch across the walls of the gutted auditorium, and the floor is crowded with tables piled with books: *The Wit of the Answering Machine, 1001 Great Advertising Slogans, Inflate Your Brain.* . . . Beside the propped-up figures two young blondes deep in conversation lean against the cash-desk. 'She has the same hair as me,' one says in a voice light as tissue, and her friend responds: 'I'll have to try it sometime.' There's something rather forbidding about the perfection of their young faces, their long eyelashes and blue eyes and pink lips, their unblemished flesh; he can't help thinking of the oldest of the models on the covers of the books he has just disowned. The thought sends words blundering out of his mouth. 'Can I have one of you?'

They turn to him with expressions so identically polite that their spuriousness disconcerts him. 'I mean, can one of you show me where you keep Simon Mottershead? Not the Mottershead who has fantasies about girls of your age and younger,' he adds hastily. 'The one who wrote *Cadenza.*'

None of this has made any visible impression on them. He feels as if their perfect surfaces are barriers he can't touch, let alone penetrate. 'I'm talking about books, you understand,' he says. 'I want you to show me some books.'

The assistant to his left glances at her colleague. 'Better call the manager.'

'Is that necessary?' Mottershead says. Apparently it is; before he has finished speaking, the other girl presses a button

47

on the desk. A bell shrills somewhere behind a wall, and a woman several years older than those at the desk but made up to look the same age rises like a figure in a pop-up book from behind a table. 'What can I do for you?' she asks Mottershead.

'I'm waiting for the manager.'

'I am she.'

'Then you can help me,' Mottershead says, trying to sound friendly and apologetic and amused by his gaffe. 'I'm after Simon Mottershead.'

'We have nobody of that name here.'

'Books by him, I mean.'

'We have none.'

'Can you show me where to look? I believe you, obviously,' Mottershead lies, 'but you've such a large stock . . .'

The woman grunts as though he means that as an insult. 'You'd be wasting your time. I know every book in this shop.'

Why is she trying to get rid of him? He feels as if the blackness which threatens his mind is darkening the shop, gathering like smoke under the roof. His surroundings, the faces of the women included, appear to be losing depth. 'At least,' he says desperately, 'you must have heard of Simon Mottershead.'

'I won't pretend I have.'

The blackness is about to swallow everything around him except her cut-out face and those of her assistants. 'Well, now you've met him,' he almost screams, and flounders towards the exit, which he can barely locate. As he makes a grab for the door, someone who has been waiting in the doorway steps into the shop. It's the man with the false scalp.

He blocks Mottershead's path and holds up one hand, and Mottershead loses control. Seizing the man's shoulders, which feel loose and swollen, he hurls him aside. The man falls headlong, taking two of the propped-up figures with him, and Mottershead is sure he's exaggerating his fall, playing to the audience, who emit cries of outrage and run to help him up. Mottershead knocks over the rest of the propped-up figures to hinder any pursuit and kicks the door shut behind him.

He's hardly out when he sees another bookshop through the trees. Its sign – Everything Worth Reading – is so challenging that he can't resist it. Fewer bicycles are about, and they and their bells seem slowed down. He sprints between them and peers around a treetrunk. When he sees nobody following him he scurries to the third bookshop.

The frontage seems altogether too narrow for the shop to accommodate the stock of which the sign boasts. On the other hand, if the proprietor's standards are higher than those apparent in the other shops, shouldn't this one stock Mottershead's work? He pushes open the black door beside the dim window occupied by a few jacketless leathery books. A bell above the door sounds a low sombre note, and the proprietor raises his head.

His black hair looks spongy and moist as lichen. His whiskers bristle on either side of his long pointed face. He's sitting behind a scratched desk bearing an ancient cash register and a book catalogue, the corners of whose pages have turned up like dead leaves. His wrinkled eyelids rise lethargically as he stares at Mottershead, who strides forward and sticks out his hand. 'Simon Mottershead. *Simon*,' he emphasizes to ensure there's no mistake.

The man gives the hand a discouraging glance and seems to brace himself as though his instinct is to recoil from his visitor. 'Whom do you represent?'

'Myself,' Mottershead says with a laugh which is meant to be self-deprecating but which comes out sounding wild. 'I'm the writer.'

'Which writer?'

'Simon Mottershead.'

'Congratulations,' the bookseller says with a distinct lack of enthusiasm. 'To what do I owe such an honour?'

'I was wondering which of my books you might have.'

'I can hardly tell you that if they haven't been published.'

'They have been,' Mottershead wails, struggling to recall titles which will help him fend off the blackness that seems about to consume him; he feels as if he no longer exists. '*Cadenza*. Even if it's out of print, you must have heard of that one.'

'No must about it, I fear.'

The shop is much longer than was apparent from outside: so long that its depths are almost lightless. The growing

50

darkness might be the absence of his books made visible. 'Let me tell you the story,' he pleads, 'and perhaps it'll come back to you.'

The bookseller stands up and gazes past him. 'You'll have to excuse me. I've a customer.'

A moment later the bell tolls. Should Mottershead take advantage of the diversion and search the shelves for his name? Finding it in the face of the bookseller's denials would be the greatest triumph he can imagine. He edges past the desk and glances at the newcomer, and darkness rushes at him. 'He isn't a customer,' he says in a throttled voice.

'If he's about to make the same approach to me,' the bookseller says, 'I must ask you both to leave.'

'Of course he isn't,' Mottershead manages to articulate, rather than lay hands on his pursuer. 'How could he?'

The bookseller opens a drawer of the desk and reaches into it. 'Please leave or I'll have you excluded.'

'You already have,' Mottershead says bitterly, and lurches towards the exit, away from the tunnel of blackness which the shop feels like. The bald man is in his way. The top of his scalp is concave now, dented by his recent fall; his eyes have grown luridly bright, perhaps as a result of pressure on his brain. 'You're a witness,' Mottershead appeals to the bookseller, whose hand is still in the drawer, gripping a weapon or a telephone. 'I've told this creature to stay away from me, otherwise I won't be responsible for my actions.'

The bookseller shakes his head. 'Please fight outside.'

Mottershead sees himself and his tormentor as the bookseller is seeing them: two unpublished and probably unpublishable writers, mutually jealous because of their lack of success. The unfairness appals him, and he's about to make a last attempt to persuade the bookseller of his authenticity when the bald man distracts him. 'I've got something of yours,' he says with a secretive grin.

'Whatever it is, you're welcome to it. Keep it as your fee for leaving me alone,' Mottershead tells him, thinking that it must be the damaged copy of *Cadenza*. Since the other doesn't move, Mottershead lunges at him, and is gratified to see him flinch and cover his scalp with both hands. 'Stay away or you'll get worse,' Mottershead snarls, and marches out of the shop. Then his confidence deserts him, and he flees towards the open space beyond the avenue.

He won't stop for anything, he promises himself. The prospect of failing to find himself in yet another bookshop – of prolonging the black depression which seeps through him like poison – terrifies him, and yet he's unable to refrain from scanning the shopfronts in search of one more bookshop, one more excuse to hope. Didn't he behave like this when *Cadenza* was published? Was that the day when he flustered from bookshop to bookshop, feeling as though just one copy of the book would convince him he existed, until he was ready to do anything that would stop him feeling that way? He's dismayingly grateful that there seem to be no more bookshops on the avenue. Nevertheless a window causes him to falter: the window of a clothes shop.

He's past it – past the full-length mirror among the shirted torsos and bodiless legs dressed in kilts or trousers – before he knows what he has seen. He wavers, stumbles onwards, backtracks reluctantly. He sees himself reappear in the mirror, walking backwards like a figure in a video cassette playing in reverse. Under his suit, which is so faded that its pattern has vanished, he's wearing only a singlet full of ventilation holes through which the grey hairs of his chest sprout: neither a shirt nor socks.

So this is the image of himself which he has been presenting. No wonder everyone was leery of him. His reflection is beginning to tremble before his eyes; his helpless rage is shaking him. He's staring at the mirror as if he is hypnotizing himself – he's unable to look away from the sight of himself among the portions of bodies arranged like a work of art composed of dismemberment – when the man with the dented scalp appears behind him.

The reflection shivers like disturbed water. The movement seems to spread beyond the mirror, causing the torsos and severed limbs to stir as if they, or the single dusty head which lurks in one corner of the window, may be dreaming of recomposition. Perhaps one day he'll be able to derive a story from all this, Mottershead thinks desperately, but hasn't he already written something of the kind? His legs are pressing themselves together, his crossed hands are clutching his chest in an attempt to hide the discoloured flesh. The other cranes over his shoulder, and Mottershead feels as if he has grown a second head. 'Just a few words,' the man whispers moistly in his ear.

'Suck a turd,' Mottershead howls and staggers out of reach, bumping into the window as he twists around to face his pursuer. 'Will those do? Will that satisfy you?'

The man rolls his eyes and licks his lips. Perhaps he's trying to adjust his teeth, but he looks as though he is asking for more. Mottershead shouts every insult and obscenity and combination of them he can think of, a monologue which seems endless and yet to need no breath. When at last he runs out of words, his victim hasn't even flinched. He raises one hand to his mouth to shove his teeth into place and gives Mottershead a disappointed look. 'That didn't sound much like a writer.'

'Then I can't be one, can I?' Mottershead says with a kind of hysterical triumph. 'Happy now?'

The other reaches for his teeth again as a preamble to responding, but Mottershead won't hear another word. He knocks the hand aside and digging his fingers into the man's mouth, seizes the upper set of teeth. The tongue pokes bonelessly at his fingers but can't dislodge them until he has taken the teeth, which he shies across the avenue, narrowly missing a lone cyclist. 'Fetch,' he snarls.

His victim gapes at him as though the weight of his jowls is more than his jaw will sustain. Though he quails at the thought of encountering the tongue again, Mottershead plunges his fingers into the open mouth and grabs the lower set of teeth. Plucking them off the blackened gums, he throws them as high as he can. They lodge in the branches of a chestnut, startling a bird, which flaps away along the avenue. 'That should keep you busy for a while. Don't even dream of following,' he warns, and runs after the bird.

Ahead, beyond a junction which puts an end to the shops, parkland stretches to the horizon. The sky above the park is cloudless, as though cleared by some emanation from the cropped grass. Here and there clumps of trees shade benches, all of which are unoccupied. As Mottershead passes the last shops the bird soars and seems to expand as it flaps blackly towards the zenith. Then it shrinks and vanishes before he expects it to do so, and he squeezes between two of the rusting cars which stand alongside the park.

The gates are held open by bolts driven deep into the path, cracking the concrete. Each of the stone gateposts is carved with a life-size figure which embraces the post and digs its face into the stone as though trying to hide or to see within. Above the scrawny limbs and torsos, the bald heads are pitted and overgrown with moss. Once he is through the gates Mottershead glances back, but the faces aren't emerging from the parkward sides of the posts, even if the moss on each of them resembles the beginnings of a face. Nor can he see anyone following him.

Beyond the gates the paths fan out. Most of them curve away between the benches, but one leads straight to the horizon, which is furred with trees. As Mottershead strolls along this path he seems to feel the city and everything which has befallen him withdrawing at least as far as the limits of the park. The grass is green as spring and sparkles with rain or dew, drops of which flash like windows to a microscopic world. He won't stop walking until he reaches the trees on the horizon, and perhaps not then unless he has grasped why the park is so familiar.

He's beyond the outermost of the benches when he begins to remember. He was walking with his family, his wife holding his hand and their son's, their daughter holding Mottershead's other hand. Shafts of misty sunlight through the foliage started the trees singing. He felt as if his family were guiding him, keeping him safe while his dreams took possession of the woods. He felt that he was being led towards the fulfilment of a dream he didn't know he had. Perhaps he was incapable of believing in it or even of conceiving it while he was awake.

In that case, how can he glimpse it now? Too many impressions are crowding it out of his head. Is it a memory, or could it be something he wrote or intended to write? Whichever, he feels certain that he recognizes the setting – that he has walked with his family through the woods at the far side of the park. They had a house beyond those woods. Isn't it possible that his wife and children still live

54

there? That would mean he has a chance to make it up to them.

He can't think what he needs to put right, but surely he'll remember when he comes face to face with them. Did he use them in a story in some way that distressed them? He begins to jog towards the woods and then, as the trees remain stubbornly distant, to run. He seems to have got nowhere when he stops dead, having heard a toothless voice call his name.

He whirls around, snarling. The sky overhead seems to shrink and blacken, the clumps of trees appear to stiffen, clenching their branches. He can see nobody except a woman dashing through the gateway, dragged by three obese poodles dyed pink and green and purple, each dog wearing a cap and bells. Then the voice calls again, its speech blurred by the lack of teeth. 'Here you are.'

His tormentor must be hiding among the nearest clump of trees; Mottershead's rucksack is lolling on the bench they shade. He would happily abandon it, but if he doesn't confront his pursuer he's liable to be followed all the way to his family's house. He stalks towards the bench.

The man isn't in the trees around it. Mottershead can only assume the sight of the rucksack attracted his attention to the wrong clump. He grabs the rucksack and wriggles his arms into the straps, feeling a weight which must be the damaged copy of *Cadenza* settle on his back. 'Thank you. Now please go away,' he shouts.

The only movement is of the poodles, which are rolling on the grass near the gates so zealously that they've dragged their owner down with them. As Mottershead stares about, he notices that all the houses bordering the park sport television aerials. Was he on television? He seems to remember cameras being poked at him, lights blazing at him, technicians crowding around him. How many people saw him on their screens, and what did they see? Not knowing makes his surroundings feel like a concealed threat. 'Stay away from my family, you lunatic,' he cries, and runs back to the straight path.

He feels as if the contents of the rucksack are riding him, driving him towards the woods. Whenever he passes another clump of trees around a bench he scrutinizes them, though when he does so they appear to draw themselves up, to become identical with the previous clump. He's dizzy from peering around him and behind him by the time he reaches the end of the path.

Two trails lead from it into the woods. One is wide, and ribbed as though outlined by a giant ladder half buried in the earth. The other winds through a thicket, and he takes it at once, trusting the trees and the undergrowth to betray any attempt to pursue him.

The thicket is more extensive than he anticipates. The trees blot out the sky with branches so closely entangled that it's impossible to tell which foliage belongs to which. The leaves of the shrubs which mass between the trees, narrowing the path, look starved of sunlight; some are pale as the fungi which swell among the roots. Roots encroach on the gloomy path, so that he has to keep glancing down as he sidles through the thicket, peering ahead for the end.

At first he's able to ignore the way the darkness seems to creep closer around him whenever he examines the path, and then he tells himself that it's bound to grow darker as he progresses. But the darkness feels like a sign of pursuit – it feels like a sack which someone is poising over his head. Glaring over his shoulder, he sees that the thicket has closed in behind him, obscuring the view beyond it so thoroughly that the park and the city might never have been there at all.

Though he can neither see nor hear anyone pursuing him, his sense of being followed infests the woods. Foliage gathers overhead like eternal night, fungi goggle at him from beneath the mob of shrubs. He can't keep glancing back, because many of the shrubs between which the path meanders are full of thorns on which he's liable to tear himself. When he fixes his attention on the way ahead, however, he has the impression that he's allowing a pursuer to gain on him – that the dented head is about to crane over his shoulder, protruding its eyes and its discoloured tongue. 'Stay out of my mind,' he whispers, grabbing at branches and letting them whip savagely past him.

He feels as if he has ventured into a maze of thorns whose points are catching at his mind. He's tempted to retrace his tracks, but when he turns he sees that the branches which he let fly have blocked the path, rendering it indistinguishable in the gloom. At least the way ahead is passable, since initials and whole words are carved on the trees beside the path.

He's less inclined to welcome these signs of life once he succeeds in identifying the words. A tree to his left is inscribed vertically with one word: SOCKETS. A flap of bark has been left hanging from the next tree as though to expose the words DREAM OR SCREAM. Most disconcerting is the message displayed by a trunk on the opposite side of the path – NEARLY A TREE – because when he surveys the woods beyond it, several of the trees seem unconvincing, more like wood carved and assembled to masquerade as trees. He sidles between the thorns as rapidly as he dares in the gathering darkness.

The path bends sharply, and as he approaches the bend he observes that the trees directly ahead of him are carved with words from their roots to their crowns – tree after tree, leading his gaze into the depths of the woods. It seems to him that the thorny gloom must contain words enough to fill at least one book. Should he force his way through the bushes to read them? Perhaps the thorns won't injure him, for he's beginning to identify with them, beginning to think that the thorns themselves must have scratched the words on the trees; he can't imagine anyone struggling through the mass of them to do so. He feels as if the thorns aren't reaching for his mind after all, they're reaching out of it. He tries to grasp that impression, but it's too like an embodiment of the dark for comfort. He drags his gaze away from the engraved trees and edges along the path.

The woods are loath to release him. Thorns snag his rucksack and his shoulders; he feels as if the contents of the rucksack are trying to delay him. How long has he been stumbling through the woods? Will he ever be out of the dark? He's suppressing a fear that the path may have turned back on itself, because wherever he looks in order to pick his way he's confronted with paragraphs gouged out of timber. He's afraid to rest his gaze on them even for a moment, knowing that he'll be compelled to stand and read them while the darkness continues to gather.

Now the thorns ahead are rising above him as though to drive him back. The rucksack tugs at his shoulders, the thorns overhead seem to writhe. He winces from side to side of the path, convinced that he can feel thorns reaching for his eyes. His left eye twinges as if the point of a thorn has touched the surface of the eyeball, and he claps one hand over his eyes and gropes forward with the other. The skin beneath his fingernails is tingling with apprehension. No thorns have pierced his fingertips, however, when the rucksack slumps against his spine and he flounders into the open.

It's almost as dark outside the forest as it was beneath the trees. Glancing back, he sees that he has emerged through a gap in a hedge which, in the darkness, looks impenetrable. The path, or his deviation from it, has led him into the back garden of a large two-storey house.

Light from a kitchen window and between the curtains of the adjacent ground-floor room lies on the worn grass, trapping him in the intervening darkness. He's preparing to dodge through the narrower ray and sneak around the building to the road when he recognizes the house. The curtains may not be familiar, but the gap-toothed look of the arch above the curtained window is, and the tilt of the bricked-up chimney and the droop of the handle of the back door. This was once his house.

The gap in the hedge was his doing. No wonder he was able to place the woods; they were his refuge whenever he found that he couldn't think in the house. He remembers taking care to leave the thorny branches intact, to make it harder for anyone to follow him. He remembers returning from the woods one day to find his children carving their initials on the kitchen doorpost, glancing fearfully towards him as the hedge creaked. His wife ran through the kitchen to rebuke them before he could lose his temper, but listening to her reasoning with them was more than he could bear. 'Give me the knife,' he said to her, and saw the blade flash in all their eyes. 'Maybe one day people will know this was where we lived.'

The initials are there on the jamb, all four sets of them. The pile of final letters appears to depict a steady hum, a lullaby which he can almost hear and which makes him

58

feel dreamy and safe, home at last. The situation isn't so simple – he can't assume that he will be received with open arms – but surely once he sees his family he'll recall what happened in the interim. He creeps along the track of darkness, grinning in anticipation of the sight of their faces when they become aware of him. He's halfway across the lawn when a man appears beyond the gap between the curtains of the downstairs room.

Mottershead throws himself flat. The lawn feels like a mattress hardened by age, prickly and full of lumps. Is the man a burglar or some even more dangerous intruder? Mottershead gropes around himself in search of a weapon and finds a rake, its tines upturned a few inches in front of him. If he'd taken one more step before prostrating himself they would have had his eyes. He draws the rake towards him between the strips of light and begins to raise it through the shadow so as to grasp the handle.

The rake is perpendicular in front of him when he wonders if the man, who has passed the gap between the curtains, may be in the house by invitation. He can't assume that, he has to establish that his family is unharmed and not in danger. He has been pressing both hands on the tines of the rake in order to lift the handle; now he lets go with one in order to reach for it. His other hand can't support the weight, and the rake totters. As he tries to grab it with both hands, it falls into the light with a thump and a clang.

He digs his hands and face into the soil and lies absolutely still. The curtains rattle, the light spreads over him, and then the sash of the window bumps up. 'Are you all right, old chap?' the man calls. 'Stay there and we'll get you.'

Mottershead seizes the rake and hauls himself to his feet. The man, who has a long face and a mane of reddish hair, looks concerned until he sees Mottershead clearly; then he frowns. 'I lived here,' Mottershead gabbles. 'I'm just going.'

'No hurry, old fellow. Perhaps you still do. Come round the front and we'll see if we can find your room. Shall we put the rake down? It's a bit late for gardening, don't you think? When it's light we can see about finding you your very own plot to look after.'

Mottershead lets the rake drop. His embarrassment and discomfiture are giving way to panic, but he has to be certain that he's right to leave. 'My wife and children aren't still here, are they?' he says as calmly as he can manage. 'The Mottersheads.'

'I'm sure they'll be here at visiting time. Let's go round the front now and I'll let you in.'

Mottershead makes himself stroll to the corner of the house. As soon as it conceals him he breaks into a run, intending to be past the gates by the time the nurse opens the front door. But he slows to glance through the window in the side of the house.

Beyond the window is the dining-room. All the furniture has been replaced. About a dozen old folk wearing plastic bibs which cover their chests are seated at a trestle table draped with cellophane. Brawny nurses of both sexes stand behind them, spooning greenish slop into their toothless mouths or removing slices of bread which two of the diners have placed on their own heads. One nurse seems about to knock with her knuckles on a balding woman's skull but desists, simpering, when she catches sight of Mottershead. He puts on speed again, too tardily. As he rounds the house, the male nurse opens the front door.

He raises his long face towards Mottershead like a hound on the scent. 'Sorry to have bothered you,' Mottershead calls to him, backing towards the gates. 'I should be somewhere else by now. I'll be on my way.'

The man's face seems to elongate as his mouth opens. 'We've someone who's a bit confused here. I don't think we want him wandering off.'

He's addressing two of his colleagues, who have just stepped into the drive. Their eyes gleam with the light of the streetlamp outside the gates; the rest of their faces are covered with surgical masks. They move to either side of the drive and advance on Mottershead like mirror images, each stretching out a hand to take him by the arms.

He waits until they're almost upon him, his neck twitching as he watches them over his shoulder. At the last moment he dodges around them, leaping and nearly falling over what's left of his wife's rockery, and dashes across the car park

which most of the front garden has become. He swings himself around an upright of a sign naming the Wild Rest Home and manages to drag the right-hand gate open as the concrete catches at its bolt. Struggling through the gap, he clashes the gate shut and looks back.

The nurses have already caught up with him. Though he didn't hear them following, all three are close enough to touch. The eyes of the masked nurses are far too large; their masks are so flat it seems impossible for them to be concealing any features. Their companion's face points like a hound's towards Mottershead, and he poises himself, eager for the chase, as they each seize one of the gates. 'Stay,' Mottershead cries, and flees into the dark beyond the streetlamp.

Has he strayed back into the woods? Surely the suburban street ought to lead to a main road, but he's having to dodge around trees which sprout thickly from the pavement and even, it seems, from the roadway. There must be houses; he sees the flickering of televisions, though their screens appear to be among the trees themselves rather than in rooms. If he has turned the wrong way at the gates, it's too late to rectify his error. The single lamp has already been blotted out by trees dripping with mist, but he knows his pursuers are behind him. He runs towards the sound of an engine revving somewhere ahead.

It's a bus, and he doesn't care where it's going so long as it helps him escape. When he glances round he sees that the nurses are gaining on him, the long-faced man's nose quivering above the bared teeth, the others flanking him, their lack of faces glimmering. The sound of the engine is moving gradually to Mottershead's left, and he sprints in that direction, trying to avoid the patches of unsteady light where he glimpses figures watching televisions, unless the shapes are monumental statues which have collapsed in front of marble slabs. Then the long-faced nurse draws level with him, leaping over the source of one patch of flickering, which seems to freeze him for a moment so that Mottershead can see him clearly: face like a hound's skull, pallid flapping belly, limbs white and thin as bones. He drops to all fours and bounds ahead, ranging back and forth while he waits to see which way Mottershead will dodge.

Mottershead runs straight at him, praying that will make him falter. Instead the man leaps to meet him, his eyes bulging as whitely as his teeth. Mottershead lurches aside and puts on a final desperate burst of speed, which takes him away from the sound of the bus. There are no lights where he's running, only trees which loom in front of him whichever way he stumbles. 'I won't go back,' he tells himself, unable to say it aloud for the clamping of his jaw, feeling as though even his voice has deserted him. He swerves around another tree and another, and suddenly he's in a narrow passage where weeds and branches overhang the high walls. He dashes along it, tripping over bricks which have fallen from the walls, and at last it lets him into the open.

He's on a street which winds between dark dumpy houses. All the houses are derelict, as are the cars parked beneath smashed lamps along both sides of the road. Nevertheless the street isn't entirely lifeless; he hears the creaks of rusty springs, and several bunches of heads rise to watch him through the glassless windscreens, their tiny eyes glittering like raindrops. He peers along the brick passage, which for the moment is empty, and tries frantically to judge which way to run. The groaning of the engine becomes audible once more, and the bus grinds into view between the houses to his right.

The vehicle is dark except for its guttering headlamps. He stares at the passage again and sees three figures racing towards him, stretching out their arms until it seems they could finger the ground without stooping. He forces his way between two cars, and feels them shake as he disturbs their occupants. He staggers into the road, waving his hands wildly at the bus.

Is it really bound for somewhere called Frosty Biceps? He hasn't time to reread the destination, he's too busy trying to catch the attention of the driver, who is bent so low over the steering-wheel that his forehead appears to overhang his eyes. The driver sees him and lifts his expressionless face, whose features are squashed into a concavity between the jutting forehead and prominent chin. The vehicle slows, and Mottershead digs in his pocket for the envelope of money.

The bus halts a few feet away from him and the door wavers open.

He hasn't reached the platform when the vehicle starts to trundle forward. Glancing behind him, he sees hands drumming their fingers on the walls at the end of the passage, three hands on each wall, as if his pursuers are only waiting for the bus to forsake him before they run him down. 'Help me,' he pleads.

The driver doesn't brake or look away from the road, but his forehead and chin relax sufficiently to let him open his mouth. 'Get if you're getting,' he mutters.

Mottershead clutches at the metal pole beyond the door and hauls himself onto the platform. At once the bus sways around the next curve, barely missing two derelict cars and almost throwing Mottershead off. He hangs onto the pole until the door drags shut like a curtain rusty with disuse, then he takes one hand from the pole to reach for the envelope. 'Ferry?' he says hopefully.

'You'll end up where you have to go.'

The driver seems to begrudge him even that response. Mottershead wraps his legs around the pole, feeling like a monkey, and tries to hold the envelope steady while he inserts a finger beneath the flap. 'How much is it?'

The driver jerks his head, vaguely indicating the depths of the bus. 'You'll have to deal with him.'

Presumably he's referring to a conductor, but the vehicle is too dark for Mottershead to locate him. No doubt he'll come to Mottershead, who clambers upstairs as the bus sways onwards. As soon as he's on the top deck he clings to the banister above the stairs and peers through the grimy windows.

The passage down which he was chased is already out of sight, and the road is deserted. Otherwise the view behind him and ahead of him is less reassuring. The spaces between the houses are piled high with refuse: crumpled cars, bent supermarket trolleys, handless grandfather clocks hollow as coffins, huge verdigrised bells, television sets with doll-sized figures stuffed inside them, their faces and hands flattened against the cracked screens. He can't tell whether the hulks beyond the houses closest to the road are buildings or abandoned buses. He staggers to the front seat and falls into it, sitting forward to let the contents of the rucksack settle themselves, and then he sinks back.

There's movement above him. A round mirror is set in the ceiling over the cabin, allowing the driver to survey the top deck through a spyhole. Having spied Mottershead, the driver returns his attention to the windings of the road, and Mottershead looks back. As far as he can distinguish in the thick gloom, he's alone on the upper deck. He gazes ahead, willing the landing-stage not to be far.

He rather wishes he hadn't noticed the mirror. Its bulbousness stretches the driver's forehead and chin so that his dwarfed eyes and nose and mouth appear to be set in a crescent of flesh surmounted by a tuft of whitish hair. The feeble headlights flicker over the derelict suburb, and Mottershead has the impression that the houses themselves are stuffed to their roofs with refuse; certainly the figures in the gaping windows are being thrust towards the sills by the tangled masses within. As the bus swings around a curve, scraping several cars, he thinks he sees a figure lose its hold on the second-floor sill where it's perched and fall head first onto the concrete. He can't be seeing all this, he tells himself; it's just that he hasn't had a chance to recover from the day, from the effect which the man with the unreal pate had on his mind. Another figure plummets from a window, the impact flinging its head and all its limbs in different directions, and he realizes that the figures are dummies. He shouldn't even be watching, he hasn't sorted out his fare. He tears open the envelope and brings it to his eyes.

It contains half a dozen coins and several folded notes. As he pulls out the notes and smooths them on his palm, the coins rattle together. Surely he has misheard the sound. He leafs through the notes, peering so hard at them that his vision shivers, then he glares at the coins. All of the latter are plastic, and apart from a note in some unrecognizably foreign currency, the notes are from a board game too.

He clenches his fists in helpless rage, crushing the notes, splintering the coins. So the writers' group never held a collection for him. The man who handed him the envelope must be responsible for its contents, and Mottershead is certain now that the man has been doing his best to drive him mad. When did he begin? He followed Mottershead into the room in the library, but from where? Perhaps from the bookshop where Mottershead found the copy of *Cadenza* – perhaps from the bedroom which Mottershead thought was a bookshop. The further back he tries to remember, the further and deeper the madness seems to reach; it's like a black pit into which he's falling with increasing speed. Then a glimpse of movement jerks him back into full awareness of his situation, and he glares at the mirror.

At first he thinks it may have been only the driver who moved. The man's face looks more misshapen than ever, the brow drawn further forward than the chin by the globular mirror. Beyond him, however, Mottershead can just discern the reflection of the lower deck, which is no longer empty. Some way down the aisle there's a hint of a face in the air, a glimmering of eyes and teeth.

The eyes and the grin must be dismayingly large to be visible at such a distance in the dark. They look deserted by flesh. He can see nothing of the head they occupy except for a pale scrawny blur, but he sees movement below them, in front of them. It has begun to reach two hands towards the stairs.

It's as though the mirror is a transparent egg inside which an embryo is forming. That image seems to clarify his vision, and he thinks the eyes are about to hatch or otherwise transform. Though neither the head nor the blur which is presumably its body has advanced, the thin white hands are much closer to the stairs. He can't tell whether the spindly arms or the hands themselves are lengthening, but he feels as if his seeing the shape is allowing it to reach out – as if his inability to look away or to stop seeing is attracting it to him. His fists close convulsively on useless paper and plastic. He shies everything he's holding at the mirror and scrabbles in his pockets. As the last of the notes flutters to the floor he finds the sharp portions of his broken credit card.

He takes them out and holds them between fingers and thumbs. There's one blade for each of his eyes. In the mirror the huge unblinking eyes above the knowing grin watch him. He lifts the points towards his face, trying to take aim despite the tremors which are spreading from his fingers to the rest of him. He'll have to apply the blades one at a time, he thinks. He tears his gaze away from the mirror, from the sight of the driver crouching over the wheel as if determined to ignore the presence in the aisle, the hands which appear to be drawing the rest of it towards the stairs. Mottershead grabs the back of his own head so that it can't flinch out of range, and poises the first blade in front of his left eye.

The bus has arrived at the brow of a hill, where the houses come to an end. Beyond the last ruins, whose walls are almost buried in refuse, the road snakes down a bare slope into blackness. At the foot of the hill is a looming mass relieved only by a few lit windows. His thinking is so constricted that at first he doesn't understand why the two lines of windows, one above the other, are identical. The lower rank is a reflection in black water; the windows are those of a boat.

Dare he risk heading for the stairs if that means the shape in the aisle may touch him? He'll never reach the ferry otherwise. The point wavers in front of his eye, his hand grasps the back of his skull. The bus accelerates downhill, and the sudden movement jerks his head towards the blade. With a choked scream he opens both hands just in time for it to scrape his cheekbone.

The plastic skates across the floor and clatters down the stairs. He still has a weapon, if such a defence will be any use. He mustn't imagine the worst or he'll be lost. The bus is more than halfway down the slope. He shoves himself off the seat and turns towards the stairs, bracing himself to confront what may be waiting at the bottom. But it isn't there, it's in the aisle behind him.

The rudimentary face grins with delight. The thin white fingers are visibly lengthening, and he has stumbled almost within their grasp. They're moving not so much like fingers as like the legs of spiders dangling in the gloom. If he hadn't stood up when he did they would have closed over his eyes. That thought and the sight of them paralyses him, but another swerve of the vehicle throws him forwards. A convulsion of panic sends him sideways, where he manages to duck away from them, onto the stairs. He's two steps down when they swoop over the banisters and touch him.

They touch his eyes. They feel like tongues composed of material softer than flesh. He hurls himself backwards, colliding with the metal wall, hacking at them with the blade. In the moment before they recoil from his attack he seems to feel a fingertip penetrating the surface of each eyeball. Blinking wildly, he slashes at the fingers as they retreat. Their substance tatters like wet paper, and he wonders if any of it is left in his eyes. As the remnants of the hands shrink back over the banister he staggers downstairs, moaning in his throat. 'Stop,' he screams.

If his plea has any effect on the driver, it causes him only to mime indifference. As he leans over the wheel, his features seem to retreat into the hollow between his forehead and chin. Mottershead lunges at the door and wrenches at the handle. Either as a result of his violence or because the driver has released the mechanism, the door folds inwards, but the vehicle maintains its speed. It swerves towards the landing-stage, which consists of no more than a few planks embedded in glistening mud. The bus is travelling so fast that it almost skids onto the planks. The driver brakes, and Mottershead seizes his chance. As the bus slows momentarily, he launches himself onto the stage.

His impetus carries him across the planks at a helpless run. They shift alarmingly, sliding sideways. Some of them aren't even set in the earth, they're floating in water which looks thick as mud. Before any of this has registered he's stumbling headlong onto the ferry as it bumps against the stage. By grabbing at the banister of the staircase which leads to the upper deck, he manages to halt himself. He clings to the rusty metal and stares back.

The bus is veering up the hill. Nothing appears to have followed him or to be about to follow. Though he can't hear or feel the working of the engine, the boat is drifting away from the stage, several dislodged planks of which are trailing in its wake. He feels hollow with relief, and so the boat is some way out before he notices that it has ceased to show any lights.

Could the crew have abandoned it while he was on the hill? Even being cast adrift seems preferable to his encounter on the bus. All the same, he would like to see where he's going. He scrambles upstairs to the top deck.

Several benches stand by the rail on either side of the deck. Ventilators rise above them, fat pipes whose wide mouths are turned towards the rail. Two pairs of double doors lead to a lounge below the wheelhouse. The sky and the water might be a single medium, a stagnant darkness which coats the surfaces of the vessel and fills the lounge and wheelhouse. He sits on a bench and watches the ruined suburb on the hill withdraw like a stage set and sink as though the blackness is consuming it, and then he sits and waits.

He isn't sure what he's waiting for: perhaps for daylight, or the appearance of another shore, or – best of all – of another boat with a crew to take him on board. He hopes he won't have to wait long, because it's beginning to prey on his nerves; he feels as if he isn't alone on the boat after all. The doors to the lounge keep stirring furtively as if someone is peeping between them. That could be due to the motion of the vessel, though its rocking is imperceptible, but what has he begun to glimpse in the mouths of the ventilators, ducking out of sight whenever he glares at them? Whatever is keeping him company, everything seems to conceal it; even the benches, which remind him increasingly of boxes with concealed lids. Perhaps the lids are about to shift. Certainly he senses movement close to him.

He grabs the rail and pulls himself to his feet. As he stares about the deck in the midst of the shoreless water he feels something dodge behind him. He presses his spine against the rail. The deck is deserted, but something is behind him. He's about to twist around until he catches sight of it, even though his instincts tell him that he won't succeed, that he'll go on spinning until he can't stop. Instead he makes himself stay as he is, and grips the rail to hold himself still. Before long he senses movement at his back.

He knows where it is. He might have known sooner, he thinks, if it hadn't been infecting his perceptions. He shoves himself away from the rail and strides to the middle of the deck, an expression which feels like a grin breaking out on his face. Planting his legs wide to steady himself, he shrugs off the rucksack and dumps it on the end of a bench. As he unbuckles it, the contents stir uneasily. He pulls it wide open and stoops to peer within.

69

There's no book inside. The only contents are a naked doll about two feet high. Though it's composed of whitish mottled plastic, it looks starved and withered. He inverts the rucksack, and the doll clatters in two pieces to the deck, the unscrewed top of the skull rolling away between the benches, the limbs twitching as the rest of the doll sprawls. What has emerged from the head scuttles into the depths of the rucksack and tries to burrow into a corner. Mottershead slams the rucksack onto the deck and stamps on it until the struggling inside it weakens and eventually ceases, then he kicks it and the doll overboard.

He hangs on to the rail and gazes at the water. Something is reluctant to let go of him. It feels like teeth buried in his brain, gnawing ratlike at its substance. As sluggish ripples spread through the water the teeth seem to burrow deeper and to lose their sharpness. The ripples fade as the doll and the rucksack sink, and he feels as if a toothless mouth has lodged in his skull, its enfeebled tongue poking at the fleshy petals of his brain. The ripples vanish, and so does the kiss in his brain, as if the mouth has been starved of brain matter. Now that his mind is clear he turns to see where the boat is approaching.

It's an island covered with trees and illuminated faintly by a crescent moon. Is it the place which feels as much like a dream as a memory? He has dreamed of being guided through the forest, following shafts of sunlight which appear to be both marking out his path and lingering on secrets of the forest: trees inscribed with messages of lichen; a glade encircled by mounds composed of moss and tiny blossoms as if the processes of growth are performing an arcane ritual; an avenue of pines whose trunks, which are straight as telephone poles, are surrounded by golden flakes of themselves as though sunlight has solidified in the piny chill and settled to the earth. Surely all this is more than a dream, despite his impression that the forest never ends – and then he sees that the ferry has brought him home.

The prow is pivoting towards the stage where he embarked before dawn. He can just see the avenue of poplars which leads to his house. Couldn't the forest which seems to cover most of the island be the source of his vision? There's no telling in the dark. At least the vessel isn't drifting aimlessly; someone is in the wheelhouse after all, steering the boat to the shore.

As the ferry nudges the stage Mottershead descends the stairs. Since there's nobody to moor the craft, he waits until the hull scrapes the tyres at the edge of the stage, then he runs at the gap where the gangplank should be, and jumps. The ferry swings away at once and sails into the blackness, but he has time to glimpse the helmsman. Is it the bearded sailor from the earlier ferry? He's wearing a Balaclava, though he seems to have pulled it down over the whole of his face. If its dim silhouette represents the outline of the skull, then surely Mottershead ought to have noticed how odd the shape was. It's the fault of the darkness, he thinks, or else his perceptions aren't as undistorted as he has allowed himself to hope. He'll feel better once he's home. He turns away from the water and strides towards the house.

The poplars creak and sway as though they're about to collapse beneath the burden of the low thick sky. All the houses among the trees are unlit, and he can't locate any of them by the glow of the moon, within whose curve he seems to glimpse a hint of features. He feels as though he can sense the growth of the forest around him; he keeps his gaze fixed on the tarmac for fear of straying once again into the woods. When he sees the lights of his house ahead he sprints towards them.

It doesn't matter that he can't recall leaving the lights on. He runs up the overgrown path, fishing for his keys, which rattle out of his pocket like the chain of a miniature anchor. He's almost at the front door when he hears a voice beyond the curtains of the lounge: his own voice.

Worse yet, it sounds terrified. He feels as if he isn't really outside the house – as if only his terror is. He's tempted to flee into the woods rather than learn what the voice may have to tell him, but if he takes to his heels now he knows he will never be able to stop. He aims the key at the lock and grips his wrist with his other hand to steady it. At last the key finds the slot, and he eases the door open.

The bulb above the L-shaped hall is lit. The hall and the uncarpeted staircase look faded with disuse. Beyond the door to the lounge his voice is babbling incomprehensibly as if it's unable to stop. He retrieves his key and creeps into the hall, inching the door shut behind him.

He isn't stealthy enough. The voice is suddenly cut off, and he hears the whir of a speeding video tape. He slams the front door and racing across the hall, flings open the door to the lounge.

Three people are sitting in the slumped armchairs: a woman who may be about his age, a younger woman, a man her age or slightly older. All have greying hair, which seems premature in at least two of them, and faces so wide that their foreheads appear lower than they should. As Mottershead strides into the room the man jumps up and snatches a tape out of the video recorder while his sister clears away a board game strewn with plastic coins and toy notes. 'Darling,' the woman says to Mottershead, 'we were just coming to fetch you.'

'We've been wondering where you'd got to,' says her daughter.

'Have you been working all this time, Dad?' the man says gently, as if Mottershead isn't already beset by enough questions of his own. Have they come to visit him, or are they living with him despite what he told the writers' group? Were they somewhere in the house when he left it, or did they let themselves in later? 'I've been using my mind all right,' he tells his son, to get rid of at least that question.

'Then I should put your feet up now,' his wife advises.

'Take it easy,' says his daughter. 'You've earned the rest.'

'Try and get some sleep,' his son says. 'We're here.'

Why isn't Mottershead reassured? Part of him yearns to embrace them, and perhaps he'll be able to once he has watched the video cassette – once he no longer feels that they're keeping a secret from him. He knows they'll try to dissuade him from watching if they realize he means to do so. 'Aren't we eating?' he suggests.

'If you're ready to put some flesh on yourself,' says his wife.

'I'll help you,' his daughter tells her, and they both go out. His son has slipped the video cassette into its case and is trying to pretend he isn't holding it. 'I'll put that away,' Mottershead informs him, staring hard at him until he hands over the cassette and trudges out of the room. 'Close the door,' Mottershead calls after him. 'I'd like to be alone for a while.'

The cassette has been recorded from a television broadcast. Handwritten on the label is the title, *Out Of His Head*. Does that refer to the creative process? Might he just have heard himself reading one of his stories aloud? Again he seems to remember cameras and lights surrounding him, but now he has the disconcerting notion that it isn't the memory which is vague – it's rather that he was unsure at the time whether the crew and their equipment were actually present. He shoves the cassette into the expressionless black mouth of the player and turns the sound of the television low as the image shivers into focus.

The cassette hasn't been rewound completely; the programme is under way. One of his books is hovering in space. *Postpone the Stone* – of course that was a title of his; why couldn't he have called it to mind when he needed to? A trick of the camera flips the book over like a playing card and transforms it into another of his novels, *Make No Bones*, and then into *Cadenza*. He's about to run the tape back to remind himself of his work when he hears what the commentary is saying about him.

'– speculate with an intensity best described as neurotic,' an unctuous male voice is saying. 'In one of his stories a man who's obsessed with the impossibility of knowing if he has died in his sleep convinces himself that he has, and is dreaming. Another concerns a man who believes he is being followed by a schizophrenic whose hallucinations are affecting his own perceptions, but the hallucinations prove to be the reality he has tried to avoid seeing. The reader is left suspecting that the schizophrenic is really a projection of the man himself.'

Did Mottershead write that? He's reaching out to halt the tape, so as to have time to think, when he sees himself appear on the screen. The sight freezes him, his hands outstretched.

He's walking back and forth across a glade – whether in the forest on the island or behind his old home isn't clear – and muttering to himself as rapidly as he is walking. Now and then he lurches at trees to examine the bark or squats to scrutinize the grass, and then he's off again, muttering and scurrying. His grin is so fixed, and his eyes are so wide, that he looks afraid to do anything but grin. Every few seconds he digs his fingers into his unkempt scalp as if he feels it slipping.

While he has been straining unsuccessfully to distinguish his own words Mottershead has ceased to hear the commentary, but now he becomes conscious of it. '– in the last of his rare interviews,' the voice is saying. 'The price of such intense commitment to his work may have been an inability to stop. At first this took the form of a compulsion to tell his stories to anyone who could be persuaded to listen. Later, immediately prior to his breakdown, he appears to have been unable to grasp reality except as raw material to be shaped. The breakdown may have been precipitated by the creative urge continuing to make demands on him after he had lost the power to write.'

He can almost remember telling stories to people in the street, to anyone who wasn't swift enough to elude him. He has the impression that the last such encounter may have been very recent indeed. Before he can seize the impression, his family enters the glade. They look younger, though their hair is already greying. They're trying to coax him home from the woods, but he keeps dodging them, both his gait and his voice speeding up. His babbling sounds more like the voice he overheard on his way in. He is still failing to understand its words when he hears his family murmuring outside the room.

He drags the cassette out of the player. He hasn't remembered everything; he's at the edge of a deeper blackness. He doesn't want to face his family until he has managed to remember. He hugs the cassette to his chest with both hands as if someone is about to take it from him. When the plastic carapace begins to crack, he's afraid that its contents may escape. He shoves the cassette into its case and stuffs the case into his pocket as he tiptoes to the door to hear what his family is murmuring about him. Before he reaches it, the voices cease.

He clasps the doorknob and presses his ear against a panel, but can hear nothing. He throws the door open, and the women turn to gaze at him from the kitchen at the far end of the hall, while his son comes to the doorway of the dining-room. 'Anything we can do, Dad?' he says. 'Want someone to sit with you?'

'I'm fine the way I am,' Mottershead retorts, wondering how they can all have withdrawn so quickly from discussing him outside the lounge. He advances on his son, expecting to find that he has only been pretending to busy himself. But the table is laid; all four places on the dim tablecloth are set, except for one from which the steak knife is missing. He knows instinctively that it's his place. 'You aren't finished,' he stammers, and makes for the stairs.

The women continue to watch him. Under the fluorescent tube their hair looks grey with dust, their foreheads appear squashed by shadows. It seems to Mottershead that they may be about to transform, to reveal their true nature, of which these details are merely hints. His mind hasn't quite cleared itself, he thinks. He mustn't let this happen, not to them. 'I'll be upstairs,' he shouts. 'No need to come looking.'

'That's right, you put your feet up,' his daughter says.

'You've earned it,' his son adds.

'Get some rest,' says his wife.

Even this unnerves him; it revives an impression of his life with them, of how it became a monotonous descent by excruciatingly minute stages into a banality with which he felt they were doing their best to smother him. Or was that something he tried to write? He dashes upstairs to his room.

He lies on the mattress and gazes at the branching cracks and peeling plaster overhead. The sight makes him uneasy, but so does the rest of the room: the shapeless bulging contents of the chest of drawers, the eternally open wardrobe, the blurred shapes in the wallpaper, where he can see figures flattened like insects if he lets himself. He closes his eyes, but shapes gather behind the lids at once. Should he switch off the light? He feels as if his sole means of finding peace may be to retreat into the dark. He hasn't opened his eyes when his family enters the room.

They must have come through the door from the corridor. Even if he sees them standing on the side of the room furthest from the door, they can't have emerged from the wardrobe.

'Having a snooze?' his son says. 'That's the ticket. We were just wondering if you'd seen a knife.'

'Why should I know where it is?'

'We aren't saying you do,' his daughter assures him. 'You have your snooze while we see if it's anywhere.'

He shouldn't have admitted that he knows what they're searching for; he feels that the admission has made them wary of him. As they peer into the wardrobe and poke through the drawers full of unwashed clothes and fumble at the heavy curtains, he's sure that they are surreptitiously watching him. He inches his hands out on both sides of him and gropes under the mattress, but the knife isn't there. Suddenly afraid to find it, he shoves himself off the bed.

The three of them swing towards him as though they are affecting not to move. 'We won't be long,' his wife murmurs. 'Just pretend we aren't here.'

'Bathroom,' Mottershead cries, thinking that he'll be alone in there if anywhere. He sprints along the corridor, past the rooms whose shaded light-bulbs steep the single beds in crimson, and into the bathroom, clawing at the bolt until it finds the socket. He crosses his wrists and clutches his shoulders as he stares around him.

The room is less of a refuge than he hoped, but at first he doesn't understand why. Is it the sound like a faint choked gurgling, not quite able to form words, which is making him reluctant to sit on the lid of the toilet or lie in the rusty bath? Though it can only be the plumbing, it seems like a memory, or at least reminiscent of one. His gaze roams the bathroom and is caught by a gleam beside the sink: his open razor.

If he's made to feel trapped in the room, he doesn't know what he might do. He scrabbles at the bolt, to get the door open before his family starts murmuring outside. The door bangs against the wall, and the heads crane out of the other rooms. His children appear flayed by the crimson light behind them, his wife's hair looks matted with dust; they seem to have hardly any foreheads. The sight appals him, and he flees past them, flinching out of reach. There's still somewhere he thinks he may be safe – the locked room.

The key was in the lock earlier, but suppose it has been removed while he was wandering? As he runs downstairs and along the corridor, he feels as though his nerves are all he is. He glances into the dining-room in case the knife has reappeared, but now the other knives are missing too. Even seeing the key in the locked door doesn't help; indeed, he wants to rush out of the house and never come back. But his hand is reaching with uncontrollable smoothness for the key. He turns it and pushes the door open, and switches on the light in the room.

A thought arrests him on the threshold of the bare room, which is so brightly lit by a shadeless bulb that it seems to contain nothing but illumination. Does he mean to lock the door in order to keep his family out, or himself in? Have they hidden the other knives from him? His vision begins to adjust, and he sees the walls white as blank pages, glaring like the walls of an interrogation room. Someone is lying on the floorboards under the bulb.

He can't immediately distinguish who it is, but he thinks that whoever has been persecuting him and his perceptions has managed to hide in the room. Since they are lying where the light is brightest, why can't he see them clearly? It occurs to him that he may not want to see. At once, before he has time to cover his eyes, he does. His family is in the room.

They're lying face up on the boards, their hands folded on their chests. His children's heads are nearest the door, his wife's feet are between them. At each of their throats a book lies open, pinned there by one of the knives driven deep. Their faces look as if someone has tried unsuccessfully to pull and knead and pummel them into a semblance of calm.

For a moment he believes they're watching him, though their eyes are dull with dust. But he's unable to waken any life in their eyes, even when he grabs the flex and moves the light-bulb back and forth, making their eyes gleam and go out, gleam and go out. Falling to his knees achieves nothing; all he can see is the book at his wife's throat. He finds himself reading and rereading one sentence: 'As a child he hoped life would never end; when he grew up he was afraid it might not.'

He's rather proud of having phrased that. Did he once write about doing away with his family, or wasn't he able to write it? In either case, having already imagined the act and his ensuing

grief may be the reason why he feels empty now, and growing emptier. He feels as if he's about to come to an end. Anything is preferable to the lifelessness of the room, even the kind of day he has been through.

He rises unsteadily and wavers to the door, where he switches off the light. That seems to help a little, and so does locking the door from the outside. 'I'm better now,' he mumbles, and then he shouts it through the house.

There's no response. He can't blame them for hiding from him while the fourth knife is at large, but if they'll only stay with him they'll be able to ensure that he doesn't find it first. He runs through the ground floor, hoping to meet them in each room, switching off the light in each to remind him where he has already looked for them. He darkens the stairs and runs up, he turns off the lights in the bathroom, in his son's bedroom and his daughter's. Now only his and his wife's room remains, and mustn't he have had a reason to leave it until last? 'Surprise,' he cries, starting to laugh and weep as he throws the door open. But nobody is in the room.

He stares at the desertion, one hand on the light-switch. Even the meagre furniture seems hardly present. If he finds the knife he'll use it on himself. Why does the thought seem to contain a revelation? He clutches at his eyes with his free hand as if to adjust his vision, then he gazes ahead, barely seeing the room, not needing to see. He'll never find the knife, he realizes, because he has already turned it on himself.

Perhaps only he is dead. Perhaps everything else was a story which he has been telling to keep himself company in the dark or to convince himself that he still has some grasp of the world. He has to believe that of at least the contents of the locked room. No wonder his search for his family has shown him empty rooms; dreams can't be forced to appear. At least his instincts haven't failed him, since he has been darkening the house. He needs the dark so that his story can take shape.

He turns off the last light and pacing blindly to the bed, sinks onto the mattress. The room already seems less substantial. He lies back and crosses his hands on his chest, he closes his eyes and waits for them to fill with blank darkness.

If he lies absolutely still, perhaps his family will come to him. Hasn't he tried this before, more than once, many times? Perhaps this time there will be light to lead them into the endless sunlit forest. It does no good to wish that he could return to a time when he might have been cured of his visions – when he was only mad.